'It really is the most beautiful place on earth,' Ru...

'You've told me a million times how beautiful my island is,' Fernando laughed.

'Yes, but you take it all for granted because you live here. You didn't even wax lyrical about that incredibly romantic island we could see from the cliff top at the cape.'

'No, my romantic eyes were somewhere else.'

Dear Reader

Bon día — hello, and welcome to Majorca! Our choice of island this month is ideally suited to those of you who crave sun, sea, sand. . .and sizzling romance! This lovely spot in the heart of the Mediterranean draws thousands of lovers year after year, and we are sure that Natalie Fox's exciting story will more than account for its appeal. So pack your suitcases, fasten your seatbelts and prepare to embark on an unforgettable journey. . . *Adéu*!

The Editor

The author says:

'I lived in Andalucía for five years so the Spanish people and the way of life are dear to my heart. I loved Majorca for its variety and beauty. I adore rugged landscapes, mountains, blue, blue sea and spectacular sunsets, the almond blossom in the spring and the shady olive groves. I also crave good food and wine and dazzling nightspots where you can dance till dawn. You can shop till you drop in Palma, and yet find peace and quiet to read or talk or take time out just to indulge yourself with your lover.

I truly feel that Majorca is in my soul, in my heart, my '*duende*'.

Natalie Fox

★ TURN TO THE BACK PAGES OF THIS BOOK FOR *WELCOME TO EUROPE*. . .OUR FASCINATING FACT-FILE ★

LOVE OR NOTHING

BY
NATALIE FOX

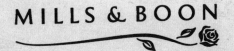

MILLS & BOON LIMITED
ETON HOUSE, 18-24 PARADISE ROAD
RICHMOND, SURREY TW9 1SR

First published in Great Britain 1993
by Mills & Boon Limited

© Natalie Fox 1993

Australian copyright 1993
Philippine copyright 1993
This edition 1993

ISBN 0 263 78281 6

Set in 10 on 11 pt Linotron Times
01-9311-57409

Typeset in Great Britain by Centracet, Cambridge
Made and printed in Great Britain

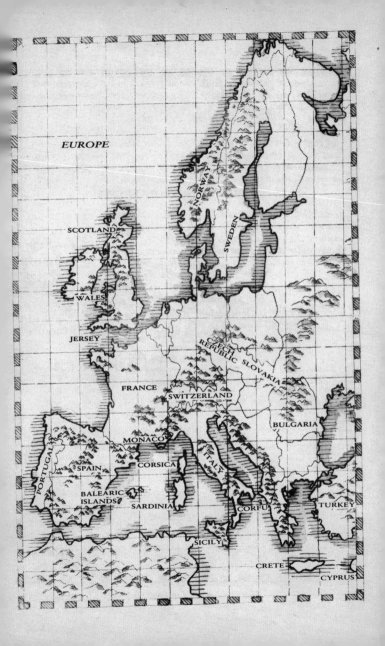

CHAPTER ONE

HE WAS tall. That was the first thing Ruth noticed about him. Head and shoulders above everyone else in the Guadalquivir suite of the Seville hotel where Iberia International Airlines were holding a promotional cocktail party.

Ruth was standing by the window, isolated by intention, gazing out at one of the seven bridges built for access to the Seville Expo site. She had turned as he entered, as if some mystical outside force had willed it. Their eyes met and Ruth's fingers tightened around the stem of her champagne glass — a defensive gesture as always when she caught the eye of a seriously good-looking male.

Business came before pleasure in her life now and instinctively Ruth's eyes flicked from the stranger to her partner Steve Cannock across the crowded room. He offered no support. Business usually came before pleasure to Steve as well but tonight was an exception. Expo fever, Ruth had put it down to as Steve had been bowled over by the exquisite beauty of an air stewardess and, forgetting that the idea of being here was to make European contacts for their agency, had resigned himself to some enjoyable flirting.

Ruth turned back to the fifth-floor window as the stranger appeared to be heading her way. Yes, he might be a useful contact but somehow she sensed he might be more trouble than he was worth.

'Beautiful raven-haired women who don't circulate at cocktail parties hold a strong fascination for me,' came the smooth voice behind her. 'You don't look bored and with a dress like that you are certainly not

7

shy. . .' She turned in time to see his warm dark eyes rake down the shimmering black silk dress that whispered around her slender body. He smiled, putting her at ease because it wasn't a lustful look that forewarned trouble. 'But perhaps you are not real, like everything else in Seville at the moment, a fantasy being created to send sane men out of their minds.'

Ruth laughed, her bright blue eyes glittering with amusement. 'And with a line like that I wonder if you're real yourself?'

Their eyes locked again but because of the closeness of him now Ruth couldn't break the contact. Oddly she didn't want to. He was different.

'How did you know I was English?' she asked softly.

His look deepened and the corners of his well-defined mouth turned up in a half-smile of mystery. '*Duende*,' he said softly. 'You have an indefinable spirit, something that only the best Spanish poets, flamenco dancers and artists are gifted with.'

Ruth's eyes widened and she couldn't help but smile. 'Ah, but you don't know that I'm not a poet, a flamenco dancer or an artist.'

His wide smile was perfect and dazzling and very unnerving, 'But I do. If you were you wouldn't be here.' His dark eyes directed to beyond the window where the Expo lights sparkled colourfully into the distance. 'The world's exotica is over there, parading for all the universe to see, and you are here. . .'

'So I must be English?' she teased.

He bowed his head to whisper tantalisingly in her ear. 'And you are.' He made it sound as if she was indeed gifted with something indefinable.

'And you, *señor*, you are obviously a warm-blooded Mediterranean, but. . .' she paused and her eyes danced mischievously '. . .you are. . .' she let her eyes travel the length of *his* body '. . .dare I say it. . .taller than most of your kinsmen.'

He laughed and took her hand and kissed it lightly. 'It is a peculiar fact of life that since tourism came to España the average height of our nation has increased dramatically. Once we were peasants on one meal a week, now we are happy to eat every day.' His voice was light and teasing and Ruth couldn't help laughing.

'But that doesn't explain your stature, *señor*,' she teased on a smile. 'You have never been a peasant, I'm sure.'

He laughed quietly. 'Maybe I owe my stature to reaching for the stars, then.' He was still holding her hand and once again lifted it to his lips to brush his mouth across the back of it. '*Querida*,' he breathed softly. 'Tonight I think I have finally captured one.'

Slowly Ruth withdrew her hand from his. His touch was warm and soft, as were his incredible eyes, hooded now with something she recognised but could do nothing to deny. She felt the chemistry and remarkably made no attempt to fight it. She'd believed herself still to be battle-scarred by her broken engagement and now was immune to such flirtation, but this man planed flirtation to a smooth, silky art she found it difficult to resist. But resist she must, because this was Seville, a new glitzy Seville that defied credibility.

With a hesitant smile she turned away from him, and sipped what was left of her champagne and gazed out of the window. A laser show from the lakeside of the Expo lit the velvet darkness of the Andalucían sky. Every secret of life and the universe was out there. The future and the past of the world was gathered on an island for everyone to see and speculate with awe. There were structures that defied gravity, fountains and sheets of cascading cool water that by night were vistas of colour and brightness that filled the heart with pulsing excitement.

She had all that to fill her heart with but at this

moment all she could think of was that the stranger had left her side. She felt the loss and wondered at it.

Suddenly the empty glass was taken from her hand and another was put in its place. She felt the coolness of the fresh glass and looked at the stranger who stood beside her once more.

'Shall we start again?' he suggested quietly. 'Fernando Serra.'

Ruth smiled. 'Ruth Appleton,' she told him.

Their voices were the only ones in the room. *They* were the only ones in the room. Ruth moistened her dry lips, feeling this Fernando moving into her secret world and not having the strength to shift him out of it. She wanted to move the conversation along as she would do with any other person she had just met at a cocktail party, to talk of work and why they were there and if they could be of any use to each other. That was the whole object of such gatherings. She must try. . . she must.

'Are you. . .are you with the airlines?' she asked.

He smiled as if he knew that had been a struggle to get out but he didn't make it more difficult for her.

'No. I own the Serra chain of hotels in Majorca.'

'On, so. . .so you're a Majorcan?'

He nodded. 'I'm here for the Expo and to promote my hotels; and you?'

'Part work, part pleasure. My partner and I ——' she nodded in Steve's direction and Fernando glanced across the room and immediately brought his eyes back to hers, but now they were darker and not so warm ' — we have our own incentive travel marketing company,' she went on, wondering at the change in his eyes. But the man was a romantic and probably saw Steve as an obstacle he might have to overcome. She could smile inwardly at that. There was nothing romantic about their relationship. They were business partners and very good friends which was a bonus and that was all. 'Steve and I teamed up a while back. We were both in the travel business and neither of us much enjoyed working for someone else. We pooled our knowledge and resources and formed our own company. We arrange incentive travel packages for companies who want to reward their salesmen for increased sales. It's very interesting work.'

'I'm impressed,' Fernando told her. 'So you are here in Seville for part work, part pleasure. So now I know the work but I don't know the pleasure.'

'The Expo.'

'Is that the only pleasure?' he asked suggestively.

He was such a charismatic man that Ruth couldn't take offence at that. 'Yes, the only pleasure,' she told him softly yet firmly.

He smiled and lifted his champagne glass to his lips and Ruth expected some sort of challenge thrown out but none came and a strange feeling percolated inside her, almost disappointment, but she shooed away the notion. She wanted no involvement with men in a romantic way. Business was more rewarding than a relationship. It had started out as a panacea for one failed relationship and had quickly become a relationship in itself. She loved her work, passionately.

'What do you think of it?'

She blinked with confusion. 'Think of what?'

'The Expo.' He raised a dark brow as he said it, as if wondering where her thoughts had been.

Ruth laughed. 'I can't take it all in,' she told him and then let out a deep sigh and gave a small shrug of her shoulders. 'It overwhelms me. I went yesterday for the first time. Steve was meeting someone in Seville and I just went on my own. There was so much.' She laughed at her own silliness. 'Too much. I ended up sitting by the lakeside and letting it all drift over me.'

He watched her as she sipped her champagne and

then his hand moved to under her chin. His touch was warm and sensual and her heart stilled.

'It shouldn't be rushed,' he told her quietly, his thumb caressing her chin. 'Like all the good things in life, it shouldn't be hurried.'

Ruth felt her throat go dry and for a moment her body yielded to something she would rather not have recognised—a need for another sort of passion in her life. Her eyes flickered her uncertainty and Fernando withdrew his hand; Ruth was grateful for that.

'You need a guide,' he suggested. 'Would you allow me to show you the way?'

The suggestion was beautifully delivered without a hint of a double edge. But she didn't know this man. He could be genuinely offering her his guidance around the exposition or he could be offering her guidance in the art of something else!

Ruth's eyes sought out Steve as if he had the answers she needed. He looked in her direction and they exchanged smiles and Ruth somehow felt that if Steve thought she was in trouble and needed bailing out he would come over immediately. But he didn't. He glanced briefly at Fernando and, satisfied that she was in safe hands, turned back to the lovely air stewardess.

'He can't help you,' Fernando said smoothly. 'The decision must come from your own heart, *querida*. It's not such a very hard decision to make, is it?'

Her eyes darted back to his and she studied him before parting her lips to give him her answer. She studied the fine features of his face, the cut and texture of his near-black hair, the firmness of his bronzed skin. There was no doubt about his looks or his manner. His whole being was a pleasure to the eye and to her senses. Minutes they had been together and yet she felt that if he walked away out of her life now she would feel a loss that couldn't be explained.

'No, it isn't difficult,' she told him softly, and it

wasn't. It was remarkably easy because she wasn't the
sort of woman to be star-struck so easily and quickly.
Was she? 'I'd like that very much,' she added.

He smiled and there was no triumph, only genuine
pleasure that she had accepted his offer, and Ruth
knew in her heart that she had nothing to fear from this
man.

They didn't speak for a very long time. They just
stood watching a fireworks display across the bridge at
the Expo. At some stage she was aware of his cologne.
At some stage she was aware that something had
happened but wasn't sure what. At some stage she was
aware that the room around them had emptied.

'We shouldn't be here,' Fernando said quietly beside
her. 'We should be over there, starting our lives
together.'

He took her hand but this time he didn't raise it to
his lips. He lowered his head and his warm mouth
brushed across hers. The contact was brief but sensual
and enough to melt Ruth's heart. She didn't move away
but allowed the small pressure to seep through to her
very soul where it nestled comfortably. Something was
happening and it was so pleasurable she didn't want it
to fade. Her eyes were only very slightly glazed as
Fernando Serra tightened his grip on her hand and led
her out of the Guadalquivir suite.

'I can't believe all this,' Ruth breathed as she let
Fernando lead her to a table by the lakeside. She
slumped down, near to heat exhaustion, and raked her
jet hair from her temples. She waited till Fernando had
ordered drinks from the waiter and then leaned across
the table that was mercifully shaded by a pergola
covered in scented jasmine and passion flowers.
Fernando sat down and leaned towards her, taking her
small hot hand in his. The contact was more than either
of them could bear, and it wasn't to do with the heat.

They drew apart, Ruth blushing, Fernando half closing his eyes in sufferance.

'What can't you believe, *querida*?'

'All this.' She waved her hand outwards and upwards. 'The Expo. It's too incredible for words. Every day, all night, it never stops. Concerts, fiestas, laser projections ——'

'And this is only our second day,' Fernando laughed.

'I should be working,' Ruth suddenly said seriously.

'So should I.'

They both laughed and didn't care.

The first night after the cocktail party had been the start of it all. Fernando had taken her to the *Zarzuela*, the Spanish operettas that had taken her breath away. She had been breathless ever since. Delivering her back to her hotel at five in the morning, he had taken her in his arms in the lobby, not caring if the world witnessed his kiss. His lips had shown a passion and need that had equalled her own but he had not pressed it any further.

Yesterday had been frantic. They had visited the fifteenth-century pavilion, which had taken them back to the world of 1492 and immersed them in an era that led up to the discovery of America. Then on to the British pavilion with its glass façade that was miraculously curtained by an eighteen-metre-high sheet of water. They had wandered the walkways that were cooled by underwater streams occasionally erupting into pools where people lingered to talk and catch their breath. They had sat by the lakeside and watched Viking longboats racing through the still waters of the man-made lake. As night fell they had turned their backs on the rush and excitement of the Expo and returned to the old Seville where they had dined by candlelight in a small pavement café and watched the world rush by.

Again in the early hours of the morning Fernando had returned her to her hotel and, cupping her face in his hands, had kissed her tenderly. She had responded by wrapping her arms tightly around his neck.

'*Querida*,' he had murmured in her ear, and Ruth had waited breathlessly for the words she hoped to hear—that she meant something to him, that he needed her, that he wanted to love her. 'Are you happy, *querida*?'

Ruth had nodded and smiled and Fernando had kissed the tip of her nose. 'Tomorrow will be happier,' he'd whispered and then, lowering his mouth to hers, he had kissed her once more before turning away and leaving her.

And tomorrow *was* happier, and different. Ruth had felt it from the moment he had picked her up at the hotel and once again they had headed for the Cartuja site of the Expo. Now, as they sat across from each other at the shady table with the heady scent of jasmine sweetening the hot air, Ruth know that it couldn't go on like this much longer.

The waiter brought them cool beers and before drinking Fernando reached out and clasped his hand over hers.

He said very quietly, 'I love you.' His eyes burned with it and Ruth's heart thudded till the sound filled her ears.

She clasped his hand and smiled across at him. 'I know,' she breathed.

'Do you now?' he smiled. 'And how do you know?'

Her eyes were bright with happiness. 'It had to be.'

'Yes, it had to be,' he echoed softly.

Slowly Ruth formed the words in her own heart. Words she thought she would never say to another man. Strangely they came easily because it was all so right. She gave no thought to what the future might hold, because this was a different world of now.

'I love you too,' she said warmly.

They drank their beers and smiled at each other and

in the distance they heard a street procession wending its noisy way in their direction. There was no interest now in what the Expo could offer them. They had each other and it filled their hearts.

Nothing needed to be said, no plans to make. They finished their drinks and as they got up from the table Fernando plucked a sprig of jasmine from the pergola. He held it under her chin and lowered his mouth to hers.

Ruth was still clutching it tightly in her hand as later he closed the door of his hotel suite behind them, locking out the world and turning to draw her into his arms.

His lovemaking was the best, the perfection she expected from such a gentle and caring man. His tender, almost lazy exploration of her body swelled her love till she felt that if she died at this very moment she would have lived her life to the full.

Her body was a new one under his sensual caresses, reborn for this man who held her heart. It was lovemaking as it should be, unhurried, uncaring of the past or the future, tender and yet deeply impassioned.

His body was a sculpture of muscled perfection; his expertise in what he did with it had her breathing with wonderment. She moved with him, matched his exploration, touched him intimately till his kisses grew more feverish. His deep, deep penetration of her came when they could hold back no longer, when the sensuality had swollen so painfully inside them that it cried out for release. Trembling with ardour, he thrust again and again and Ruth closed around him, drawing him deeply into her. Their climax came as the flaming sun dipped low over the old city of Seville. A blaze of glory, a fury of passion that left them weak and trembling in each other's arms.

Later Fernando grazed the moisture from her brow

with his lips as he gathered her into his arms once
again.

'I want to make love to you forever,' he grated,
moving his lips down to her throat. His hand ran lightly
over her breast and Ruth bit her lip with ecstasy as her
nipples engorged with desire and anticipation. She
parted her lips for him as his mouth closed over hers
once again and refused to consider where forever might
end.

The days were too short and the nights rushed by in a
whirlwind of passion. Ruth wanted it never to end but
always in the back of her mind was the thought that it
must.

Her affair with Fernando superseded everything.
Thankfully Steve was totally enraptured by the beautiful Maria Luisa so Ruth didn't have him on her conscience. On the few occasions when Fernando had some
pressing business to attend to she was able to put her
own mind to work and make a few valuable contacts
for the agency but the majority of her time was spent
with her love.

Their visits to the Expo became less frequent,
Fernando now wishing to introduce her to the romance
of Seville itself. They visited the huge Gothic cathedral
and gazed in awe at the beautiful Murillos — *Saint
Anthony* and the *Immaculate Conception* — the stained-
glass windows and the many other treasures the centuries had gifted the cathedral with. They wandered parks
and gardens and fed already overfed white pigeons in
the Plaza de América. They laughed and talked and
sipped *sangría* and ate prawns on café terraces and
watched the world walk by.

Some days when the city heat was too oppressive
they drove out into the wild Andalucían countryside,
high up into the hills where the air was sweet and pure.
The tranquil white-washed villages were a welcome

relief and they stopped at small bars and quenched their thirst with local wine and spring water.

'Is Majorca like this?' Ruth asked one afternoon as they sprawled under a shady carob tree, hot and exhausted after climbing up through the narrow streets of a village to find a goat track that led up a hillside to a secluded olive grove.

'It is greener and cooler and a thousand times more beautiful and you will see it all for yourself one day,' he told her, gathering her into his arms and teasing her lips with his own.

Would she? she wondered as he drew her into his special world of sensuality. A fleeting thought that soon she would have to return to the real world played at her conscience but as always Fernando's lovemaking vanquished such uncertainties from her mind. He was her real world.

'Oh, Fernando, this is lovely!' Ruth exclaimed.

'Do you mind?'

Enraptured, Ruth gazed around his hotel suite. The main room was awash with bowls of pink and white carnations, the sweet, peppery scent filling the room. The table on the balcony beyond was set with silver and crystal and candles burned languorously in the heat of the night.

It was their last night and Ruth turned her misty eyes to Fernando. 'It's perfect,' she breathed. She would have hated to share their last moments in a crowded restaurant. But no, this couldn't be the end. They had never spoken of the future and what would happen when their time was through but they would, because a love so consuming couldn't just end this way.

They ate delicious seafood on the balcony and tender chicken in a smooth almond sauce and they drank champagne in the moonlight as the Seville nightlife erupted below them. It was almost idyllic.

Ruth could feel the tightening of her heart as Fernando gathered her into his arms, his kisses more urgent as the time slipped perilously away. His love-making was different this time, more intense, more assertive as if he was trying to exert some power over her. Confusion ran riot in Ruth's heart. They loved each other and it couldn't end, but. . .

As always they lay exhausted in each other's arms, their sated bodies languid and limp, Fernando soothing her fevered brow with tender kisses of love.

'Stay with me, *querida*. Don't go back to England,' Fernando breathed, curling a strand of her glossy jet hair possessively around his fingers. 'I want to take you home with me, to Majorca, to be in my life forever.'

Biting her lip, Ruth tightened her arms about his neck and buried her face in his shoulder. Desperately she fought back the tears, not knowing why they had formed so swiftly. He wanted her and she wanted him but. . .she couldn't think straight. . .she was confused . . .it had all happened so quickly, too quickly.

'I love you, Fernando,' she told him in a hoarse whisper, 'you must believe that. . .'

She felt him tense beside her, only slightly but enough for her to know what he was thinking. She wanted to explain that they needed more time but of course there wasn't more time, not immediate time.

'I'm bound to my partnership,' she told him quietly, inwardly struggling for every word of explanation but not even sure what she was trying to explain. She couldn't just leave Steve in the lurch after all they had done to get the business together.

'Is this really to do with your partnership,' he grated, 'or are you just afraid of failure once again?'

She couldn't look at him. She smoothed her mouth against the firmness of his shoulder and tightened her arms around him. She wasn't even sure about that. She had told him about her broken engagement and how

deeply hurt and wary she had felt after it. But she had
given it little thought during this time with Fernando.
He had filled her heart with new hope and love and yet
. . .and yet she burned with uncertainty now.

Slowly Ruth ran her hand across his chest and pressed
her lips to his flesh once again. There were no words to
explain how she felt but her body would smooth a way.
As she felt the urgency of his body next to hers she
blanked off the uncertainty and the fear. Fernando
loved her and he would lead the way, make the decision
for her. She didn't know how he would do it but she
felt sure he would.

CHAPTER TWO

DEATHLY pale, Ruth sat next to Steve as they prepared for take-off. Steve sat as mute as herself but she was so wrapped up in her own misery that she didn't question why he was so quiet.

She had expected Fernando to turn up at the airport with his arms full of red roses and promises. Dear God, was she out of her mind? It had been an affair, nothing more. It was over.

Ruth squeezed tight her eyes and swallowed hard as the aircraft soared up into the sky. But it wasn't over because he would come after her. Fernando Serra loved her and wouldn't just let her disappear out of his life forever. She had hesitated but he couldn't take that hesitation as a refusal. He would think about it and understand and he would come after her. . .

Ruth stirred restlessly on a canvas sun-lounger on the balcony of a Palma apartment. Now, a year later, she knew her hesitation had been the biggest mistake of her life. She should have stayed with Fernando, she should have had faith in her own feelings at the time—and his. Her only excuse was that it had happened so quickly— too quickly. A whirlwind affair set against the romantic backdrop of the Seville Expo in southern Spain that by the law of averages hadn't really stood a chance from the off.

Sometimes over the past year she had wondered whether if Fernando had mentioned marriage it would have made any difference. But he hadn't, of course; he had just pleaded with her to stay with him, which was a world away from a total commitment. She also won-

21

dered if she had put him off by telling him of her
previous engagement and how wary of love it had left
her. And it had, till he had entered her life and changed
her whole way of thinking. She had been wary before
but now she was paranoid about the whole concept of
relationships. There had been no man since Fernando
and there never would be. Her work was more important to her now than ever.

Ruth flinched as droplets of water landed on her bare
midriff. For an instant she wallowed in fantasy land and
imagined that when she opened her eyes Fernando
would be towering over her and not Steve. After all,
they were on the island of Majorca, Fernando's
home. . . She sighed and lazily opened one very blue
eye and squinted up at her partner. . .so much for
fantasies.

'Painful, is it, to see me enjoying myself?' she murmured sarcastically.

'Agony,' he grated, depositing a dripping ice cube
back into a cold drink and handing it to her.

Ruth swung her long tanned legs to the patio and sat
up in the lounger where she had been soaking up the
sun lasciviously for the past hour and irrationally telling
herself that if Fernando Serra had really loved her she
wouldn't have let her slip away from him so easily.

Her thoughts were with Steve now. Poor love, he
was so fair-skinned he couldn't tolerate much sun and
Majorca was sunnier and hotter than ever this season,
according to him. He'd been before, this was Ruth's
first visit. Ruth grinned at him as he sat down at a cane
table, making sure he was under the bright green
awning that hung over the balcony and not a sliver of
sun was on the bare parts of his body.

He pulled a face at her as he shifted a sheaf of papers
towards him. 'I don't see why you should have all the
fun on these trips,' he muttered dejectedly, 'soaking up
a tan when you've already got some left from Seville

last year. Hasn't anyone warned you of the dangers of over-exposure to the sun?'

Ruth smiled to herself. She was doing all right. The mention of Seville had only aroused a small murmur of protest in her left ventricle, and that was an improvement on a few months back when open heart surgery had seemed the only cure for her suffering.

'Yes, you, frequently, piously, jealously,' Ruth teased, putting the drink down on the ground. 'It must be hell for you living with flesh that bubbles and erupts and goes a ghastly shade of taramasalata——

'OK, OK, you masochist, you!' Steve wailed. 'But don't say I didn't warn you. By the time you're thirty you'll have skin like my old school satchel.'

'So I'll worry about that when I'm thirty,' Ruth retorted, hitching up her bikini-top before loosening her long jet hair from a silk bandeau and shaking it free around her golden shoulders. She smeared after-sun milk on her satin brown skin before joining Steve at the table with her drink. She kissed the top of his head before sitting down. If only all men were like Steve—nice and uncomplicated—life would be sweet.

Ruth sipped her drink and gazed across at Steve who was happily engrossed in their latest project, a presentation for one of the largest computer software companies in the UK, offering their salesmen lavish holidays in lavish Majorca in exchange for lavish rises in sales.

They were on the lovely island putting together the whole package; visiting tourist boards, airlines, exclusive hotels, doing their utmost to get the best at the best rates for their clients. And of course having a good time. They both agreed that if you couldn't enjoy yourself on the way, what was the point in running a business that afforded them so much freedom to travel? Somehow that philosophy had soured since Seville, but neither spoke of it.

'I suppose we really ought to get down to some serious work,' Ruth suggested lazily, stretching her legs under the table and gazing out across the blue bay of Palma with its crowd of boats and yachts bobbing and, beyond, the profusion of high-rise apartments and hotels. Palm trees and the Bellver castle were silhouetted against a bright blue sky on its plateau overlooking the bay, and Ruth was impressed. It was a hot and lively capital of this popular Balearic isle of Majorca and pre-Fernando days would have found Ruth down there, twelve floors down there, getting among the hustle and bustle, soaking up the atmosphere and tasting the very essence of the island with enthusiasm.

Slowly she drained her glass and for a moment held it in front of her, staring at and smoothing the condensation away with her thumb. Funny how her life was always thought of as pre-Fernando days. Post-Fernando days were still in their infancy, even after this time, but she was trying her best. Her hand shook only very slightly as she put the empty glass down on the table.

Two days ago they had arrived at Palma airport, Steve elated at the prospect of a couple of weeks' work in his own special paradise place on earth and Ruth stuffed with foreboding. Suppose she ran into Fernando Serra again? Would she be able to cope with that after Seville?

'Yes,' she muttered, 'two days is long enough to acclimatise. I'll leave first thing in the morning.'

'Leave for where?' Steve asked, not raising his golden head from his papers.

Sometimes Ruth wished she had told Steve what had happened last year, the affair she had allowed to happen among the glitz and excitement of the Seville Expo, the fascinating Majorcan she had met and loved on sight. But Steve would have hit her with the truth — not intentionally, he wasn't cruel by nature, but simply with his down-to-earth approach to everything and everyone. Ships in the night, holiday romance etcetera, he would have sensibly suggested, and of course he would have been right. Ruth knew it but found it hard to face at times. And yet the painful burden of her love she ached to share at times, and who better with than Steve?

'Pollensa, and I'll take a look at Alcudia while I'm up there,' she told him.

'I thought we'd agreed I'd cover that region,' Steve said, giving her his full attention now, his grey eyes narrowing quizzically. 'You said you'd handle the tourist board and the airlines here in Palma.'

'No, *you* said I'd handle them and at the time I agreed but now I've changed my mind,' Ruth told him firmly.

She'd thought a lot about this since they'd planned the trip. To get out of Palma would lessen her chances of running into Fernando. He owned hotels here in the capital and further round the coast at Palma Nova and Magalluf. Pollensa and Alcudia were in the north of the island and Fernando owned nothing in that region.

'Besides, I fancy a change,' she added, raking her hair from her forehead and staring out over the balcony of the apartment. She sighed. 'I need some air; capitals stifle me.'

'Since when?' Steve laughed and directed his eyes back to the papers on the table. He didn't really want to know and Ruth was grateful for his lack of interest. It was one of the reasons they got on so well with each other. They gave each other space.

'I'm going to shower,' Ruth told him, getting to her feet and gathering up the dirty glasses which littered th table-top. 'And then I'm going to make some phone calls. I need to confirm the accommodation in Pollensa.'

Steve leaned back and stretched wearily. 'And I need some stimulus. I'll mix a jug of *sangría* ——'

'And drink it on your own,' Ruth interrupted wryly.

Sangría could have been blamed for her downfall. . .
She sighed as she padded through the spacious, marble-
floored apartment to the kitchen to rinse out the glasses
before her shower — if she didn't wash them Steve
wouldn't. *Sangría*, champagne, lakeside laser shows at
nightfall and the fabulous *Zarzuelas* — they could all
have been blamed for her downfall.

'I told you too much sun was bad for you. It affects
the brain, too.'

Dazed, Ruth looked up from the sink. Steve was
beside her, leaning across her to turn off the tap. Water
slopped over the edge of the sink and over her bare
feet.

'Where were you?' Steve asked quietly.

Ruth laughed, nervously. She was always doing this,
reliving Fernando and forgetting keys and taps and pans
on hot stoves. 'I. . .I was planning my route. . .in my
head. . .driving to Pollensa,' she said quickly to cover
her embarassment.

'Hmm, not driving to Seville?' Steve suggested drily,
bending down to mop up the water at her feet.

Ruth stepped out of his way, her breath locking in
her throat. That was the second time this afternoon he
had mentioned Seville and that was a bit of a coinci-
dence. But no, it was an association of ideas. Majorca
was Spain.

'Are we eating out or in tonight?' she asked as she
took the sopping sponge from his hand and squeezed it
murderously into the sink.

'In the circumstances I think we'd be safer out than
in,' Steve suggested cynically. 'At certain times of the
month women terrify me.'

Ruth gritted her teeth. 'And because of remarks like
that is it any wonder you're still scratching around for a
woman to share your miserable existence with?'

Steve laughed so unnaturally that it caused Ruth to
widen her eyes at him with surprise. Though he laughed

there was no matching humour in his eyes. Had she worried a raw nerve with that remark? She'd never imagined Steve to be the marrying sort but. . .

'Sorry, that was a bit of an insensitive remark to make,' she said, recalling that Steve certainly had a catalogue of failed relationships trailing in his wake. His choice, she had always assumed, but perhaps that wasn't the whole story. Maybe that Maria Luisa in Seville had meant as much to him as Fernando had to her.

'No,' Steve sighed. 'You're probably right. I deserved that. Now, how would you like to eat tonight? Chinese? Japanese —?'

'How about "when in Rome"?' Ruth grinned. 'Seafood, Majorcan-style, on the beach somewhere —'

'What about the marina, a touch of class to *launch* this project?' he quipped, adding conspiratorially, 'Company perks.'

Ruth gave him a hug and kissed him on the cheek. 'Smooth talker. Give me eight hours to get ready and you're on.'

'OK, ugly duckling, take all the time you need, but I insist on force-feeding you that *sangría* before we leave: you're as uptight as a barnacle on a boat's bum.'

Ruth was still laughing as she closed the bathroom door after her. She wasn't uptight, just a little overwrought at the thought of running into Fernando. But the island covered three thousand, six hundred and forty square kilometres, she'd read in her guide book, and the chances of running in to him must be the equal amount of kilometres to one anyway. She had nothing to fear.

'This place is superb!' Ruth enthused under her breath as the waiter escorted them to a table by the window.

'I know my restaurants,' Steve stated confidently as they sat down.

The air-conditioned restaurant was furnished beautifully in thirties chrome and pale grey velvet. The
harbour beyond was a myriad sparkling lights from
moored boats and yachts and across the bay the twink-
ling lights of Palma lit up palm trees and white tower
blocks, making them look more stunningly magical by
night than by day.

This vista painfully reminded Ruth of the lakeside
restaurants at the Seville Expo. . . No, this couldn't go
on. . .this living in the past. She cut through the heady
memories and concentrated her mind on what Steve
was saying while she watched a superb glossy white
yacht coming in to berth at the jetty not fifty metres
from the window of the restaurant.

'I know lobster is extortionately expensive here but
you know I have good vibes about this contract. . .'

Ruth stared in disbelief, her full lips parting slightly
to quicken the oxygen to her lungs. This couldn't be!
This couldn't be happening! No, she was mistaken, *this*
definitely couldn't be happening!

Ruth shifted uncomfortably in her azure crêpe de
Chine cocktail dress. Madness, but in this excruciating
moment of part-excitement, part-horror the only thing
she could think about was her wise choice of what to
wear tonight. No one seemed to dress up these days,
but tonight she had, as if. . .as if. . .

Fernando Serra, as seriously good-looking as ever,
watched from the deck as his crew tied up at the jetty.
He had always managed to look smooth and sophisti-
cated without trying and tonight was no exception. He
was dressed casually in narrow white trousers and a
white short-sleeved shirt and Ruth knew the shirt would
be silk. She could almost feel its fine, smooth texture
under her fingertips and the heat of his beautifully
muscled body through the fabric. She could easily recall
his smell too, as if he were in her arms at this very

moment—an expensive cologne warmly melded with
his very own Mediterranean muskiness.

'Steve,' Ruth murmured after the waiter had taken
their drinks order. Her heart was bleeping dully and
her skin felt moist and feverish and she needed to
talk—now. To run would be an easy option but cow-
ardly in the extreme. She was a mature, successful
businesswoman, not a gauche teenager flushing with
girlish embarrassment at the sight of a lost lover. She
was going to cope, to face this, to brave it out and lay a
certain ghost.

Steve looked up from the menu he was drooling over
and waited for her to go on. He couldn't see the yacht
from where he was sitting and Ruth was glad of that.
He couldn't see Fernando Serra and his beautiful
companion or the crew dispersing for the night. Lips
parted, Ruth watched anxiously as a waiter from the
restaurant, with a laden silver salver balanced on his
fingertips above his head, sashayed across to the yacht
at the jetty. On the salver was an ice-bucket cooling a
bottle of champagne and two long fluted glasses.
Propped between the bucket and the glasses was a
menu. They could be dining on board or coming across
to dine here later. Ruth wanted to leave but was so
panic-stricken at the thought of the latter happening
that a decision to go or stay was out of her reasoning.

'Yes,' Steve urged and Ruth blinked and gave him a
small smile. She didn't know who she felt more sorry
for—herself or Steve.

'Tell me about Maria Luisa,' she said quietly.

Steve looked as if he'd been smacked in the face with
a writ. In that moment she knew the lovely air hostess
had been someone special in his life. It was there to see
in the surprise and the pain. She wondered why she
hadn't seen any signs before this moment. But she'd
probably been too wrapped up in her own misery to
notice anyone elses. She felt a piercing guilt for that.

'What brought that on?' Steve asked after the initial shock of Ruth's request had been absorbed.

Ruth gave a small shrug. 'Being here in Majorca made me think of Seville. We've never talked about it before, the personal side of the trip, I mean. Now seems as good a time as any for some good old soul-searching.'

'Why do you want to know?' asked Steve, a little uncomfortably.

Ruth lowered her dark lashes and toyed with her cutlery. 'I just do,' she started and then stopped to draw a deep breath. 'You probably don't remember that man I was with at the Iberia cocktail party. . .'

'The guy you had an affair with?'

Ruth's eyes widened incredulously. 'How on earth——?'

'Come on, Ruth, am I mega-dumb or something? I didn't see you for days after that party——'

'And I didn't see *you*,' she said pointedly.

'So we were both pretty involved,' he said with a shrug, 'but why bring it up now?'

'I just wanted to talk about it. It. . .it was intense, the affair. We spent every minute we could together. We laughed and talked and made pretty spectacular love at every opportunity.' She let out a deep sigh of misery at the thought of all that was lost. 'And then suddenly it was all over. Our trip was at an end and it was all over.'

Steve shrugged as if it might usher the whole evening away if he was lucky. 'Look, I don't see what this has to do with me and Maria Luisa. I mean, I'll listen if you want to thrash it all out in the open——'

'I just wanted to know if you loved her,' Ruth interrupted urgently. It was important, she knew, for Steve's sake as well as her own. She wanted to know about love, a man's side of the story.

'Yes, I loved her,' Steve admitted reluctantly and then leaned back to let the waiter pour the champagne.

Ruth waited till he'd taken their food order before speaking.

'Loved, past tense—does that mean you don't love her now?' Ruth gazed past him, over his right shoulder to the yacht with its two beautiful people laughing and sipping champagne together on the upper deck. There was a warm breeze from the sea which lifted the woman's dark hair from her shoulders as she smiled and raised her chin and gazed adoringly at her companion. Ruth's eyes filled with tears at life's cruelty and she had to swallow hard to stop them spilling.

Steve reached out across the table and took her hand. 'Hey, that's not like you, looking so down and weepy.'

'No, it isn't.' Ruth smiled, squeezing his hand. 'It. . . it's just that life is so bloody and I've been carrying this dreadful emotional weight around with me since Seville and I want rid of it.' Her blue eyes widened under their dark brows. 'Steve, as well as my business partner I consider you my very best mate——'

'And you mine,' Steve told her kindly.

'—and I need to know things, if you loved Maria Luisa and still do. . .you do, don't you?' Steve nodded and she went on. 'So why, Steve?' she asked earnestly, 'Why did you let it slip out of your reach?'

Steve lifted his champagne glass to his lips and took a gulp, swishing it around his mouth like mouthwash before swallowing it. It was a habit he had that confirmed to Ruth that a romantic relationship with him could never be. If Fernando had ever. . .but he hadn't . . .and that was the pity of it all. Fernando Serra had been too perfect.

'Don't you think you ought to ask you lover that question, not me?' Steve said after lowering the glass to the damask tablecloth. 'Because it isn't my answer you want but his.'

Ruth nodded. 'You're right. But that isn't possible and you are the man sitting across from me that can help. I want a male point of view to this silly love thing we all get netted into at some time in our lives.' She couldn't help but sound cynical.

'To what end? It won't help, you know. You'll still carry that emotional baggage with you wherever you go, wondering what you said or maybe didn't say that frightened him off. But I'm a fatalist, you see. I believe whatever will be will be; that's how I cope with life. I loved Maria Luisa last year, I thought she loved me. After Seville, nothing. That's life!'

Ruth shook her dark head in dismay. 'Am I to take it that is the general male philosophy, that shrug-it-all-off attitude?'

'I can only speak for myself,' Steve opted dismissively.

'But didn't you phone her after Seville, write or send flowers? For pity's sake, Steve, you loved the girl. How could you let her go?'

Steve leaned towards her, his eyes intent and yet there was hurt there, deep hurt. 'Because Ruth, dear one, there was nothing to hold on to. Sure I phoned, left messages, the usual fool things men do in times of insanity.'

'Flowers?'

'No flowers.'

'Love letters?'

'No love letters.'

'Well, in my opinion you just didn't try hard enough,' Ruth retorted, under her breath because the restaurant was filling up now.

'I shouldn't have had to, Ruth,' he insisted. 'That's the whole point, you see. If she had felt as deeply for me as I felt for her there wouldn't be a need for all that. I did phone, several times, she was never there and I left messages. She didn't call back. She didn't care enough—fact, painful fact; she just didn't care enough.'

Ruth leaned back in her seat and clutched her hands in her lap, so tightly she was hurting herself. It was all she wanted to know really, the truth—that if Fernando had truly loved her he would have moved heaven and earth to get her back. It was a very contrary thought; after all, she had been so vague that last night together, making excuses to go back to England and honestly expecting Fernando to override them and come charging after her, exercising the caveman approach that a lot of women, in spite of their liberation, still craved— in this case Ruth, astonishingly, being one of them.

'So give,' Steve husked, obviously still feeling his loss and talking about it not helping one bit.

'What do you want to hear, a repeat of what you have just told me?'

'If you think it will help, repeat all you like.'

Ruth sighed. 'I did want to talk about it but I'm not so sure now. You seem to have filled in a few blank spaces for me.'

'Now you're making me feel bad. This was your expurgation, not mine. Talk about it, Ruth. You never know, through you I might found out the mistakes I made.'

'I don't think you did make a mistake,' Ruth told him with resignation. 'I think you did everything you could but it just wasn't enough, it just wasn't meant to be. Like me and Fernando, I suppose.

Ruth averted her eyes to above Steve's shoulder. Fernando and his lovely companion were still on board, laughing, having fun and sipping champagne in the moonlight. Such a romantic scenario, such an agonising scene to witness and yet it was compulsive viewing for Ruth. She couldn't have moved away if her life depended on it.

'Oh, God, I loved him,' Ruth breathed so

emotionally that Steve's hand came across the table to lock over hers in comfort. 'So much, Steve,' she went on in an agonised whisper. 'He was the best, the very best. He said he loved me and wanted me to stay. . .' She shook her head dismally. 'I didn't. . . I thought— Oh, I was confused, I suppose, not quite believing it was possible to fall in love so swiftly. I think what I really wanted was. . .domination.'

Steve laughed. 'That doesn't sound like you at all.'

Ruth had to smile because it certainly didn't sound like her. 'I know I can be a bit assertive where business is concerned but you know where Fernando was concerned I suppose I just went all female. I know he asked me to stay but I wanted more for some reason.' Her smile widened. 'I wanted him to chase me, not literally, though I would have been madly impressed if he'd charged up Piccadilly on a white stallion, but I just wanted some firmer confirmation that he loved me. Perhaps. . .perhaps a sweet old-fashioned proposal of marriage. It never came. He didn't call, or send flowers, or write. . .' Ruth clutched the stem of her glass and drank fiercely.

Steve grinned. 'That's my girl, get tipsy and aggressive, you know it turns me on.'

The tension was eased and they both laughed because they knew it was impossible, her getting tipsy and aggressive and him getting turned on by it.

'New theory,' Steve suggested brightly, making more effort to cheer her up. 'We weren't in love at all. We were just bowled over by Expo euphoria. If Fernando Serra and Maria Luisa were to walk in this restaurant now—'

Ruth choked on her wine and smothered a napkin over her face. This was all developing into a video nasty.

'Better now?' Steve asked, grinning widely as she finally dabbed at her eyes.

She nodded, dicing with death once again as she swallowed more champagne. 'I think you're right,' she agreed at last. 'Quasimodo could appear sensual in the right setting—candlelit dinner at the Ritz, maybe.' She giggled. 'No, perhaps not but I get your point. Seville was so exciting I suppose love in that environment was inevitable, but I have a theory too. We fell in love with a couple of Spaniards though Fernando was. . .still is a Majorcan. He said there was a difference. . . I mean between being a Spaniard and a Majorcan. . .'

She was rambling and knew it, but couldn't stop. She wasn't tipsy, just a little high, probably running a fever. The beauty had disappeared below deck now and Fernando was leaning on the handrail waiting for her and gazing out towards the harbour buildings. He looked drawn now, Ruth thought, and wondered if he had ever given her a thought since Seville. He had never been out of her thoughts, not for a minute.

'Fernando was so proud,' she went on, 'so sexy, so charming and——'

'Such a rat,' Steve finished for her.

Ruth grimaced. 'I didn't need you to tell me that but thanks for emphasising it. But if he is, so are you.'

'For not pressing my attentions on Maria Luisa?' Steve shook his head. 'Slight difference. I loved Maria Luisa and tried. Did Fernando try with you? No, not on your nelly.' He stopped suddenly, realising he was hurting her. 'Sorry,' he growled, 'that wasn't very tactful, was it? So what is this theory of yours?'

'Only that we fell in love with foreigners. Spaniards, Majorcans, Martians, whatever. They are just different, all aliens.'

Steve threw his head back and laughed out loud. No one turned and looked disapprovingly because this was Spain, one of the noisiest countries in the world. Ruth used it to stress her point.

'You see, that's what I mean. No one turned a hair

at your raucous laughter. If this were Knightsbridge they'd all be tutting like crazy now. They aren't the same. This might be Europe and we are all Europeans now but we are still different.'

'*Vive la Différence*!' Steve hooted.

Someone at the next table echoed that in a foreign accent and Ruth turned to smile at him and raise her glass in a mutual toast.

'You see,' she hissed, turning back to Steve to give him her full attention. 'That couldn't happen in England. We are all too stuffy. Fernando and Maria Luisa *are* different.'

'So what has that to do with love?'

A ragged sigh escaped from her lips and she fiddled with her cutlery again. 'I'm not sure. I just keep thinking that there must be a logical reason why Fernando let me go so easily——'

'How perverse of you. How like a damned woman. What was to stop you chasing *him, illogical* female pride?'

'Possibly,' Ruth conceded. 'But it doesn't alter the fact that Fernando and Maria Luisa just let us both go, and maybe it was to do with their culture and their ways, something we didn't understand, something we did wrong.'

Steve snorted. 'We took it all too seriously, that's what we did wrong, sweetheart. We both talk of love but those two were smarter than we took them for. They took Seville for what it was and it wasn't love. It was just one of those *flings*!'

Ruth's eyes filled with pain at the truth of that blunt statement. Love. Fernando had said and she had said, and really it boiled down to the misuse of the three most precious words in the universal language — I love you!

Steve leaned across the table and took one of her small hands in his two. 'You know, there isn't a thin line between love and infatuation. There's a socking great chasm. I've been infatuated before and it's nothing to the pain of this. I loved Maria Luisa——'

'And I loved Fernando,' Ruth insisted, shaking a curtain of silky hair around her face. And she still did. She knew it with a dragging certainty. He was out there, just beyond the window, entertaining a beautiful woman on his luxury yacht, and she felt pain, and desperation and an ache and envy she wouldn't wish on her worst enemy if she had one. Love or nothing. She had made her choice. Nothing was so very lonely.

'But I still cling to the hope that I'm mistaken,' Steve went on seriously, 'that I wasn't in love and it was in fact infatuation.' He paused, looking as desolate as Ruth felt. 'But I doubt I'll ever know for sure because I'll never see her again and only by coming face to face with her will I know the truth.'

Ruth paled and her heart seemed to miss several beats as she glanced past Steve again. Fernando and his companion were preparing to come ashore, Fernando taking her elbow to help her, the perfect gentleman as always. Very, very soon the secret of life would be revealed, and Ruth would rather know the secret of death.

'You're a fatalist, are you?' Ruth breathed feverishly and Steve looked at her curiously. 'Dear God, Steve, after tonight you're going to have to take the pledge . . .join a monastery——'

'What the devil's got into you?' Steve laughed hesitantly.

'More champagne with any luck. Did you only order one bottle?' Shakily she squeezed the last two glasses out of the bottle. 'We're going to need more, a jeroboam——'

'Ruth, you're shaking——'

'I'm going to die, Steve!' she rasped dramatically. 'I

want to die!' She closed her eyes and bit her lip and said a silent prayer to be released from this hell.

'Don't be silly, you've had too much wine, that's all.'

Ruth shook her head and opened her eyes and the invevitable had happened. They were here, in this restaurant, and Fernando was chatting amiably with the head waiter. Soon, very soon, he would be showing them to their table and there was only one vacant—reserved, of course—behind Steve.

'Steve,' Ruth whispered shakily, 'I wanted to tell you about Fernando tonight because. . .because soon after we arrived here, so did he.'

Steve raised a surprised brow and breathed in disbelief. 'He's here?'

Ruth managed a nod. 'And most likely going to sit at the next table.'

'Do you want to leave?' His hand sprang out again to clutch hers supportively.

'Too late!' she squeaked. They were coming towards them now and Fernando hadn't seen her yet; this was so awful.

'Poor darling,' Steve soothed and then he smiled in that boyish way that always cheered her up but was so terribly wasted and out of place this time. 'But you'll have to face it, sweetheart, and it might not be as bad as you think. Chin up, be brave. Time is such a great healer——'

'Don't be so bloody crass!' she hissed across the table.

Steve grinned. 'Where's your sense of humour?'

'Heading for the same place as yours when you see who he's with. Are you ready for this, Steve?'

The time had come and Ruth stood up, so nervous and overwrought she nearly dragged the damask tablecloth with her. Fernando stopped dead and his lovely, dark-haired companion nearly careered into the back of him.

Ruth hysterically thought she would like this on film because you couldn't look at three people at once in such a terrible situation without missing something.

'Fernando!' she exclaimed, over-brightly. 'How delightful to see you again. . .' Somewhere across the bay of Palma a fiesta was about to break out with the usual volley of deafening rockets to launch it on its way. 'And Maria Luisa too. Well, isn't this fantastic? Seville all over again.'

'Holy mackerel!' Steve whispered fiercely under his breath.

CHAPTER THREE

EVERYONE else in the crowded restaurant faded into the chrome and velvet. Only two people in the world existed. Ruth's one thought was bound into a tight ball of despair, but him, the man she still adored, what were his thoughts? She could only make a calculated guess; sheer horror at coming face to face with a former lover when the present one stood stiffly beside him.

Fernando's eyes were cold and expressionless once the horror and surprise had faded and as Ruth made pointless reminiscent remarks in a voice that was barely her own she saw him take a worried sidelong glance at his beautiful companion. Maria Luisa was transfixed with shock, her eyes glazed and locked on Steve's face. There was an awkward silence when Ruth managed to rein in her silly chatter and then Fernando took control.

'You must join us for dinner, of course,' he suggested quietly and turned to the waiter, but before a request for a more accommodating table was spoken Maria Luisa, to everyone's shock, gave out a sudden sob of protest and turned and fled from the restaurant.

Steve acted swiftly, excused himself and sped after her. Fernando frowned and was about to follow when Ruth reached and touched his arm to restrain him.

They looked at each other. Nothing needed to be said. Both knew that the other knew that Steve and Maria Luisa hadn't just met for the first time.

Ruth slumped down into her seat, drained by all that had happened. She didn't know what to do or say, and even if she had her body and mind were incapable of acting on it. Fernando sat in the seat Steve had vacated, turning to speak to the waiter in rapid Catalan before giving her his full attention.

'So, you are here in Majorca. What for?' His voice was clipped, uninterested in advance in her answer. It froze Ruth's already chilled heart.

'Work,' she told him quietly, her eyes seeking the dark depths of his for something that would relate to what they had once been to each other in Seville. She found nothing and it hurt so badly. She composed herself and outlined briefly her reasons for being on the island and Fernando listened, occasionally nodding.

'Perhaps I can help you. I have many contacts on the island and——'

'We have enough ourselves,' she interrupted quickly. She couldn't accept help from him. That could mean more meetings and this was hard enough to bear. 'But . . .but thank you for offering.'

'Do you make love with him?'

The question, so calmly delivered and yet so unexpected and shockingly brutal, knocked the wind from Ruth's already emotionally bruised body. A wild streak of facetiousness was all that remained.

'You mean the hovering waiter?' Her wide blue eyes swept up at the waiter as if considering him.

Fernando Serra's black eyes narrowed angrily at her and then settled on the waiter. He ordered wine and an assortment of pre-dinner *tapas* and then gave her his attention again.

'I suppose I should expect a remark like that from you, but nevertheless——'

'But nevertheless,' she interrupted brittly, 'you felt fit to ask such an irrelevant question. I haven't lost my sense of humour since last we met, Fernando, but you have.' He'd lost a lot more, Ruth noted. He was as dark and interesting as ever but he was missing a certain exuberance. She wondered if he was under business pressure.

'I see nothing humorous in suggesting my query was directed at the waiter, and nothing funny in your eyeing him that way as if the implication were a consideration. No, nothing is funny this evening, Ruth, simply extremely embarrassing.'

'Yes, it is embarrassing, isn't it?' she agreed sarcastically. 'You out with your latest mistress, running into the last, though I don't suppose I was the last. With your inbuilt tachometer you've no doubt clocked up quite a few since Seville.'

She hated herself for that, bringing herself down to a spiteful, vengeful, 'woman scorned' level. She didn't apologise, though; there was no point unless you truly regretted hurting the person your poison was aimed at. All her regrets were for herself, not him. He hadn't suffered this last year, that was obvious.

'Well, I'm sure you've broken a few speed limits yourself since then. From what I remember you were pretty quick off the starting line when the lights flashed green.'

Ruth took that because she had earned it. Somehow it was helping, this inevitable back-stabbing repartee when two lovers met after an affair that had left a pool of acid where fond memories should have rested.

'So answer my question,' he urged after the waiter had poured their wine and another had placed the *tapas* in the centre of the table. 'Do you make love with your business partner and, to prove I still have my humour, is he your sleeping partner?' He didn't even smile to warm that little joke on its way.

Ruth steeled every nerve-ending in her body. She needed to overcome the pain. 'Nought out of ten for humour, Fernando, and likewise for originality. Now my turn to be mindless: is it any of your business or even your concern *if* I sleep with my business partner?' she husked back.

'None whatsoever,' he returned coldly and then added cruelly, 'Not for my sake, that is.'

'For whose sake, then?'

'For Maria Luisa's.'

Ruth smiled wryly and forked a stuffed olive from one of the small dishes in front of her. 'And why should you show such concern over your current girlfriend's past affair? Other than for second-hand kicks, that is.' She couldn't stop, she just couldn't stop stabbing at him. And it was obvious why—pure unadulterated jealousy at meeting him again in the presence of the lovely Maria Luisa.

'I don't take my pleasures second-hand,' he told her quietly. He took up a fork and prodded at a dish of small silvery fish marinated in olive oil, garlic and wine vinegar. He looked up at her after selecting one and piercing it with his fork. His eyes were coldly hostile as he traced small circles in the air with it across the table from her. 'I made an exception once,' he said with very little subtlety, 'and it was a lesson well learnt.' He swallowed the small fish as if disposing of her very soul.

'We both learnt lessons in Seville, Fernando,' she conceded painfully. 'And made mistakes. I made one in trusting you enough to open up my heart to you about my ex-fiancé. I didn't think for a minute that if we ever met again you would so bitterly slap it back in my face with no regard for my feelings.' She was shaking as she said that; fierce little tremors of nerves shook her. Why were they being so cruel to each other? They had loved each other once, and now this.

Colour darkened his throat for a second. 'I'm sorry,' he uttered, quite convincingly to Ruth's ears but not convincingly enough for her to soften. She was still wary, very much so.

'So why so concerned for Maria Luisa's past? You obviously know she and Steve had an affair, but what it has to do with me dining with my partner I fail to see.'

'I didn't ask you if you were dining with him. I asked if you were sleeping with him, and since you have done everything to evade a straight answer I must assume the worst or the best, depending whose side you are one.'

'And whose side are you on, or is that glaringly obvious?'

'Glaringly obvious. I feel nothing for the man Steve Cannock, I feel very much for Maria Luisa. I don't want her hurt. I don't want her messed with.' His eyes hardened to slivers of jet as he spoke.

Ruth's heart went to jelly. She hadn't got a mention so fact was fact. Fernando Serra had never truly cared for her and didn't now. 'So you'd like to believe Steve is in the throes of a great romance with me?' she forced out through her hurt.

'It would delight me to know exactly that,' he aimed back at her pointedly. 'Then Maria Luisa and I can get on with our lives.'

Shakily Ruth raised her glass of wine to her lips, her heart beating despondently within her. They had a life together, Fernando and Steve's ex-love. Who would have believed life could dish up such double portions of irony?

'Well, you are free to get on with your lives,' Ruth told him quietly. 'Maria Luisa has nothing to fear from Steve.' It sounded like a veiled admission that she was romantically involved with her partner, and so be it. Fernando Serra could believe what he liked because nothing now could bring back anything remotely like what they'd shared in Seville.

'And what about you? Have I anything to fear from you?' His voice was low and softly timbred and Ruth wondered at such cruelty. This was a different Fernando from the one she had loved so passionately before. He'd changed, which was no credit to Maria Luisa. Perhaps Steve had had a narrow escape.

'You never did have anything to fear from me,

Fernando,' she told him softly, lowering her lashes to
try and hide the pain in her eyes. She stared bleakly at
the damask cloth she had traced her fingers over as if it
might hold the answer to what she should do with the
rest of her life after tonight. Post-Fernando days hit her
and they stretched interminably ahead. It was worse
than ever now. Only hours before she had been trying
to pull herself together and thinking she might be
winning; now the future was an aching black void.

She raised her lashes, raised her chin, looked him
straight in the eye through a controlled mist of tears.
'You're so concerned for Maria Luisa, does that mean
she is someone special in your life?'

'She is important to me, yes,' he answered heavily.

Self-hurt, self-punishment, she couldn't stop herself.
'And. . .and are you going to marry her?' It suddenly
occurred to her they could already be married. She held
her breath.

He said nothing, forked another fish, swallowed it
with the same indifference he might appropriate to
putting out the rubbish.

'I'm not the marrying kind,' he eventually said.

Her breath came back, softly, partly relieved that he
hadn't made the commitment with Maria Luisa, partly
saddened by what she knew already. No, he wasn't the
marrying kind. 'Nor I,' she countered, in a ridiculous
attempt to even the score. Which was very ridiculous
because it was ignored.

'But Maria Luisa and I live together,' he volunteered,
and Ruth wondered why he'd admitted to it. It would
be nice to think their affair had meant something to
him, and after Seville he was picking up the pieces of
his life and had found happiness with another woman.
It would be even nicer to think he was trying to make
her jealous because he still cared for her and not for
pure spite, and it would be nice if she sobered up and

faced life's harsh realities! Fernando Serra hadn't and didn't care a hairy monkey for her!

'I'm pleased to hear that,' she said stiffly. 'Now I really ought to be getting back to the apartment.'

'You haven't eaten yet.'

'I'm not hungry any more.' She braved herself to meet his eyes, wondering if he too had lost his appetite and for the same reason as her. This meeting was so painful.

'The apartment, do you share it with your partner?'

How wonderful if he was trying to keep her here with his questions, but she doubted that. He just had some time to spare waiting for Maria Luisa to return and why not fill it with a bit of Ruth-baiting?

'How much more evidence do you need, Fernando?' she asked tightly. 'I though we had already established that Steve and I are more than business partners.'

'Ah, but I need to know for sure, you see, because I have some doubts, and before you ask me why I should be so concerned I will assure you that this time it is partly for my own self-esteem that I would like to know.'

Ruth raised a very questioning brow and simply murmured, 'Go on.'

'I do not like Steve very much——'

'You don't know him!' Ruth retorted idignantly.

'True, I do not know him and have no wish to, but he intrigues me. I see a not very tall man, pleasant enough to look at but a beige man, not very exciting, not very sexual——'

'What are you getting at, Fernando?' she rasped impatiently.

Their eyes locked, Ruth's cold and hostile, Fernando's dark and totally impenetrable. 'What has he got that I couldn't give you?' he asked in a dull tone that chilled Ruth more than if he had bawled at her.

Ruth's toes curled under the table. If only he knew

that no man could give her what he had—thirteen frantic days of excitement and sensuality that would be with her for the rest of her life. She licked her very dry lips and refused to succumb to the temptation of another drink. If ever there was a night to be numbed by champagne this would be it, but she needed her wits with this man.

'You don't even want to know that, do you? What you want is for me to stroke your ego by telling you that he doesn't compare to you.'

At last he smiled. 'Of course. I have my pride.'

'Yes, I know and I have mine but it doesn't stretch to asking you how Maria Luisa compares to me. I consider that poor taste,' she said tartly, getting to her feet and shakily picking up her evening bag from the chair next to her. 'Now, if you will excuse me——'

'I will take you back to your apartment——'

'There is absolutely no need,' Ruth insisted. 'I know the way and it isn't far.' She didn't want to be escorted back to the apartment by him. She wanted to be alone, to cope with this shock meeting that was turning her inside out.

'The fiesta has started. The streets will be crowded——'

'I'll be all right!' Ruth said sharply, her eyes narrowing warningly. 'And don't you think you ought to wait here for Maria Luisa——?'

The waiter arrived back at the table and Fernando stood to speak to him. It was Ruth's chance to escape but the bill needed to be paid. She fumbled in her bag for her credit card but suddenly Fernando's hand was on her wrist and she was being urged out of the restaurant.

'I haven't paid——'

'Don't insult me.'

'I don't expect you to pay for my——'

'Don't expect anything out of life and you won't be

disappointed,' he growled, gripping her so tightly by her elbow that it began to ache.

'Very profound. Your own personal philosophy?'

'Since you and Seville, yes.'

Ruth nearly fell down the steps of the restaurant on to the cobbled street. Her heart was acting so erratically that she could hardly analyse what he had just said. It was the first indication from him that Seville had meant something. He was bitter and that must mean. . .but no, there was no reason for him to be bitter. If he had cared he wouldn't have let her slip away the way he had.

'This way,' Fernando grated, shifting his grip from her elbow down to her hand. 'Unless you want to end up in the Mediterranean.'

Ruth had lost all sense of direction as soon as he had gripped her hand so fiercely; she just teetered after him in her high-heeled sandals. There were people everywhere, swarming on the harbourside to watch the brightly lit and decorated boats that had appeared from nowhere and the rockets soaring into the warm night air. Small girls in long flowing flamenco dresses careered around excitedly, swirling their skirts in a parody of the fiery flamenco dances they were too young to fully understand.

'Where is this apartment you share with your lover?'

Ruth snatched her hand away from his. '*Calle del Paraiso*,' she sang back sarcastically. She was oh, so brave it was hurting.

'Living with him is paradise, is it?' he cut back equally bitingly.

'I was being sarcastic, as well you know, and it's about time you knew that Steve and I aren't — .'

A rocket exploded above their heads and Ruth screamed in terror. Fernando gathered her into his arms and she buried her face in his shirt as a volley of them erupted overhead. His shirt *was* silk and it was soft and sensual against her skin and she could feel his warmth. His smell was painfully evocative. Her teeth crunched down on her lower lip as the whirlpool of her desire sped her back to Seville when this sort of contact had been enough to. . . She pulled away from him, shakily, her eyes wide and misted, her moist lips parted in turmoil. He let her go as if he too had been dragged down by past memories.

'You . . .you'd better get back to the restaurant. . . Maria Luisa'

'My yacht is there. I'm more concerned with you at the moment,' he said roughly. 'Maria Luisa is a native, you're not. I want to see you safely home.'

Without argument she murmured the name of the apartment block, grateful for his concern. There was so much noise around them, children screaming with excitement as a fireworks display exploded across the bay. Youths dressed as demons careered across the road and yelled at the tops of their voices. Her head began to throb but it eased as Fernando guided her through the crowds to small, quieter side-streets away from the harbour.

'How long are you here for?' he asked as they walked.

Ruth kept her distance from him but she could do nothing about the wretched aura that surrounded him. He grazed through the streets as if he were some sort of god, head and shoulders above everyone. Women leaning over balconies looked and tossed down flowers, younger women openly showed their approval with a strange clicking sound and Fernando walked on, oblivious of it all.

'As long as it takes to get our work done,' she told him non-committally.

'I meant what I said about contacts. If I can do anything to help you only have to ask.'

Ruth let the tension out of her shoulders and relaxed.

This was how it should be between ex-lovers meeting
again, just normal, no animosity. How it should be but
never could be, she thought ruefully. Fernando could
never be a friend as Steve was. With the Majorcan it
was love or nothing so nothing it would have to be.

'Thank you, I'll keep it in mind.' She wouldn't.

'Do you want a coffee before you go in?' he asked.
They had reached the apartment block and there was a
café below it with white metal tables and chairs out on
the street. It was crowded with people laughing and
playing guitars and tambourines. She dearly wanted a
coffee and brandy to end this uncomfortable night but
she wanted to say goodbye and get it over with more,
and somehow the merriment of the people added to her
stress.

'No, thank you, it's late——'

'For the British.' He smiled and Ruth's heart
pumped. 'We Majorcans are just starting the night.'

That just about sized up their differences, Ruth
thought miserably. Their biorhythms were out of synch.
They lived in different worlds.

Fernando was holding out his hand and Ruth stared
down at it.

'Your apartment keys,' he urged, wriggling his
fingers.

Ruth shook her head. 'I can see my own way——'

'Keys, Ruth.'

She handed them over without any further argument.
He always had been a perfect gentleman. She followed
him to the lift, terrified of stepping into it with him and
finding it empty!

It was empty, as empty as her head had been in
Seville when she had allowed herself to fall in love so
easily.

'Where are you staying in Pollensa?'

'Pollensa?' she croaked, punching out her floor and
raising her eyes skywards as everyone did as the lift

doors slid shut. 'How do you know I'm going to Pollensa?'

'You told me, earlier on. You said your partner was seeing to the tourist board and the airlines here in Palma——'

'Yes, yes, I remember now.' Her head was muzzy, light-headed with shock, no doubt. Earlier she had come down in this lift with Steve and now she was going up with the last person on earth she could have envisaged.

They stepped out of the lift and Ruth turned to him. 'You really didn't need to come this far.'

'I've gone too far already,' he muttered cryptically as he turned away. He found the apartment and opened the door for her and stepped back to let her pass. 'Before you offer me a drink I'll decline——'

'I wasn't about to,' she interrupted quickly.

He shrugged his wide shoulders. 'I didn't think you were. It was my humour. How quickly you have forgotten.'

Her face flushed and she bit her lip. 'Yes, life moves at a fast pace these days.'

'I agree.' His hand was suddenly up above her, leaning on the door-jamb. A perfect position for bracing himself to kiss her, Ruth thought wildly in the heat of the moment. But he didn't and her heart slowed, raced, panicked and nearly died.

'Tell me something?' His voice paused, timed to raise her temperature to standby alert. 'Do you sleep well at night, *querida*?' His voice was suddenly terrifyingly husky and threatening.

'N. . .*no problema*,' she rattled so nervously she thought he must be able to smell her fear. She didn't like his tone at all; it scared her.

'You surprise me, Ruth, you really surprise me.' His voice dripped sarcasm. 'This Steve must have hidden talents. I thought I was the only one to satisfy you; you

told me that once; you said I was the only one who had
ever made you——'

'Shut up!' Ruth blurted, the tears already there, the
tears she had promised herself once this door was shut
on him.

'Does it embarrass you?' He raised an expectant
black brow. 'Once we talked of everything——'

'Once!' Ruth insisted strongly. 'Once isn't now.'

'No, now is Steve Cannock,' he grated and his hand
dropped down to his side. 'And perhaps before was
Steve Cannock too.'

'What. . .what do you mean?'

'Well, I think I'm just getting to understand how you
two operate. You are lovers now and there is a good
chance you were lovers before Seville——'

'No!'

'No? I think yes, I think you two have some sort of
arrangement to take other lovers when you feel the
need, but just a word of warning, *querida*. I don't like
those sort of games; they are hurtful and painful to
others. . .' She had hurt him, therefore he must have
cared. . . Ruth's heart lifted but plummeted when his
voice dangerously threatened, 'You tell your lover and
business partner when he returns that I will ruin him if
he ever lays a finger on Maria Luisa again. Do you
understand that?'

Ruth wanted to die. In that moment of truth she
wanted to be struck by lightning and reduced to
smouldering ashes. No, Fernando didn't like those sort
of games he was imagining, but not for himself—his
emotions were untouchable. He felt for his precious
Maria Luisa. He was truly concerned for her, and that
was something Ruth didn't want to think about.

'I. . .I'll tell him nothing of the sort, Fernando Serra,
because your problems are your own,' she husked
pityingly. 'But remember one thing before you go all
"Mafia" on Steve Cannock. He isn't home yet and nor

is your precious Maria Luisa, and for all you and I know it's already too late!'

Ruth shook inside as she watched his eyes darken furiously. His hands bunched to fists at his side. She had never seen him angry before. Her eyes flickered nervously in anticipation of the eruption of that anger.

'Then we both have a problem to deal with,' he grated roughly.

'No!' Ruth cut back bravely. 'I haven't a prob——'

'But you have!' Fernando interrupted harshly. 'Because if you don't keep your lover away from her I'll have the two of you off this island with twice the speed of those rockets out there. Have I made myself clear?'

'Absolutely!' she uttered coldly, her eyes as icy as his. She held his, defiantly and strongly, determined not to do anything of the sort. Steve's life was his own and as appalling as this situation was she was powerless to interfere anyway. But Fernando didn't know that, though she had tried to tell him that she and Steve had never been lovers. Now it didn't matter. Steve had talked of being a fatalist and if Fernando had the power to have them removed from the island that was fate and she wasn't going to fight it.

She unlocked her eyes from his and turned to pass through to the apartment. There was nothing more to do or say. Suddenly she was incredibly tired, her bones were aching and her head was sore with fighting back the tears.

Fernando Serra caught her arm and swung her back. His hand, warm and strong, took her chin and held her firm.

'Such coldness,' he breathed. 'And yet once you were warmth and sensuality. No fear of your partner doing to you what he did to Maria Luisa, because you haven't a heart. You and this Steve deserve each other. May you both rot in hell together.'

Shocked, Ruth couldn't move. There was anger and hurt deep inside her but she was so stunned by his cruelty that she couldn't rouse it in defence of herself.

Fernando lowered his head and Ruth arched stiffly against the door-jamb. Oh, God, no! She closed her eyes, braced her heart within her. If his lips touched hers she'd never be able to conceal the truth — that her love was still there in spite of his hatred for her.

There were no warm lips on hers but the warmth of something hard and unyielding. Ruth blinked open her eyes and Fernando was gazing down at her, a new Fernando, one she didn't know any more. Mockery glittered his dark eyes and there was a cruel twist to his mouth as he grazed the key to the apartment across her full, expectant lips.

'Wish that I did have the courage to kiss you, *querida*,' he rasped, 'but I have standards and a level of decency to live up to and they are more important to me than a moment of weakness to prove that I am immune to you.'

He lifted her hot hand and pressed the key into her moist palm, and as there was nothing more to say he turned and walked away, Ruth watching numbly, powerless to scream out in her own defence, powerless to feel.

Ruth finished her coffee and rinsed her cup out before writing a note for Steve. She'd already checked his room and he was sleeping soundly. She couldn't even feel resentful that he slept so peacefully after she had suffered a sleepless night of angst. Poor darling, he'd probably been to hell and back as well last night. He'd returned at dawn, creeping into the apartment so as not to wake her. He obviously hadn't wanted to talk and in a way Ruth was relieved. She wasn't ready yet and neither was Steve. They both needed time to themselves.

In the note she said she was on her way to Pollensa
as arranged and would phone him later. She made no
reference to last night or Maria Luisa. Life was going
on as planned, she told herself determinedly as she
walked down the street to the car rental office with her
overnight bag. Fernando Serra could make all the
threats he liked but he couldn't stop her carrying on her
business. He wasn't God.

Ruth left Palma and took the road to Valldemosa.
The open-topped Suzuki jeep she'd hired was easy to
drive and the breeze whipping through her hair helped
to clear her head.

His island, she mused, as she drove through almond
and olive groves. It *was* special. It was too late in the
year for the almond blossom but the valley was beautiful none the less. Majorca was renowned for its spring-
time almond blossom, Fernando had told her. He'd
told her about Valldemosa too, which was why she was
taking this route to the north of the island. Chopin had
spent a winter there with his illicit mistress George
Sand. The local people had stoned her for wearing
trousers in the street and Fernando had ruefully added
how things had changed since then — now anything went
in Majorca.

Ruth was fascinated by the charterhouse where
Chopin had composed his 'Funeral March'. His piano
had a single red rose poignantly lying across the key-
board. A bit of romanticism his mistress might have
abhorred, Ruth suspected, as she had hardly
enamoured herself with the locals, nor they with her.
Ruth sympathised with her. Mistresses had hard times.

Deiá was Ruth's next stop. Here was where all the
intellectuals and artists were supposed to hang out.
Robert Graves had made his home here and Ruth
understood why. It was a poet's dream. The pretty
village with its coloured houses and shuttered windows
and narrow streets was set among olive groves on a hill.

It seemed that here was where the magic of Majorca lay, the *duende*, as Fernando would have said. Picasso too had stayed near by in a cluster of farmers' cottages. She wondered what 'period' he had been enraptured with at the time he'd been here.

Ruth drove on to Puerto de Sóller where she stopped for refreshment on the seafront where trams rumbled behind her. It was crowded with tourists having fun in the sun and wallowing in watersports. She felt the isolation then of not being a part of anyone. She shook off the feeling with determined resolution. She would make the best of these few days up here, work and yet take time to relax and most of all to forget Fernando Serra.

'Look, this is ridiculous,' Ruth protested. 'My partner made the original booking, I know, under our company name, and I phoned yesterday to confirm the apartment. I spoke to you, I recognise your voice——'

The young man behind the reception desk at the entrance to the urbanisation shook his head adamantly. 'I think you are mistaken, *Señorita*.'

'I don't make mistakes,' Ruth protested hotly. She was really feeling tired now, half wishing she hadn't indulged herself taking in the sights. 'Look, I have a fax. . .' She fumbled in her bag. Damn, she couldn't have left it behind in Palma. She could have, easily; she could have forgotten her head after last night! 'OK,' she said resignedly, 'so there has been a mix-up in the booking, these things happen. Just rent me another apartment——'

'We are full. I'm sorry.'

Ruth stared in disbelief. Embarrassed he looked, but definitely not sorry.

'Full?' Ruth echoed incredulously. 'You can't possibly be!' She waved her hand in the direction of the open door where beyond a wilderness of pretty villas, stacked white-washed town houses and holiday apartments filled the landscape. 'You have thousands of units out there——'

'All full, *señorita*. You forget, it is the height of the season.'

Ruth paled with weariness. She needed at least three full days here and the thought of driving to and fro from Palma every day. . .no, it was out of the question . . .impossible.

'Is. . .is there somewhere else you can recommend?' she asked weakly, forcing her tangled wind-blown hair from her brow.

'I am sorry. There is nowhere. The whole of Pollensa is full. We have the music festival. . .' His voice trailed off and Ruth looked sharply at him as he lowered his gaze and looked down at the paperwork in front of him. A dismissive gesture but to Ruth one he didn't relish doing very much.

Something deep inside her stirred suspiciously, but no, it wasn't possible. She certainly *hadn't* made a mistake with the booking *and* she had confirmed it. Last night the apartment was available and now today it wasn't.

Ruth opened her mouth to protest but closed it again. Hopelessly she walked outside and stood in bright sunlight wondering what to do; a few thoughtful seconds later she knew.

Se alquila—there were several 'To Let' signs as she drove slowly through the complex and all requesting clients to apply to the central reception for details. Ruth was furious.

Fernando Serra, you are in serious trouble, she raged inwardly as once again she pulled up outside the reception unit. This time she wasn't going to be fobbed off. If she had to bribe the wretched receptionist she would. She was determined to find out the truth and act on it.

CHAPTER FOUR

IT HAD cost her, more than just a few thousand pesetas. It had cost Ruth her pride in being forced to do such a thing. Well, with any luck she'd get a fair return on her outlay, in deep satisfaction.

She drove fearlessly up a narrow dirt-track road that wound steeply between scented pine trees because she was still mad that Fernando could have done such a thing. The receptionist had opened up readily enough when Ruth had opened up her purse. Fernando Serra had instructed him to instruct her when she arrived that there was no room at the inn! How dared he?

Casa Pinar was easy to find. The private dirt track led directly to it. Ruth jumped out of the jeep at the heavy wrought-iron gates. The place was like a fortress with its high natural stone walls and the ubiquitous bougainvillaea cascading over the top if it, matching the colour of Ruth's fury — cyclamen-pink. She was just about to rattle the huge gates in fury when there was a clunk and the gates whirred open.

So much for security, Ruth mused as she leapt back into the jeep and drove up the long gravelly drive; I could be a burglar for all he knew.

She pulled up in front of the massive Moorish-style stone mansion that was Fernando Serra's home, and Maria Luisa's, of course. So far rage had propelled her here; now she'd arrived she felt queasy inside. They'd be here, together, and she couldn't bear that, but she would have to, just long enough to voice her fury.

'Houw much did it cost you?'

Ruth whirled round and faced Fernando who'd

appeared from nowhere as she was peering up at the house. He didn't look at all surprised to see her.

'What. . .what do you mean?' Her throat was suddenly incredibly dry. He wore white shorts and white vest-top and carried a tennis racket—and tennis was a game for two at least. She shouldn't have come! Her eyes flickered worriedly beyond him, looking for Maria Luisa.

'She's not here,' he told her with a mocking ring to his tone which showed he knew exactly what she was thinking. 'She's away for a few days. So how much did it cost you?'

'What?'

'The bribe.'

'What bribe?' She felt the colour rising and couldn't control it.

'Remember we had a discussion about this once— the ethics of bribery to get what you wanted. You were quite adamanat that you would do it ——'

'In a life-saving context,' Ruth retorted. 'We were talking about ransoms too and I said I would pay to save the life ——'

'You said you would pay to save *my* life,' he reminded her, his eyes glinting humorously, which made Ruth angrier than ever. 'Because you thought I was worth it.'

'Things change, Fernando. I wouldn't part with a bent peseta for your life now.'

He laughed. 'But you parted with a few to find out where I live. I'm flattered.'

She should have known that that stupid receptionist would inform Fernando, to save his own skin, no doubt. He must have been on the phone as soon as she had stormed out of the door. No wonder those gates had opened without a challenge, no wonder he hadn't looked surprised to see her. He'd been expecting her.

'Yes, I did,' she admitted defiantly. 'But don't feel

flattered. It was worth it to tell you what a toad you are. So there you are. You're a toad, a fatherless toad. I feel better already.' She raised her chin and smiled sweetly at him. 'Now I'll go back and tell that silly little receptionist what a silly little toad he is too and if he doesn't turn over the keys to the apartment that I booked and paid a deposit on I'll scream all the way to his boss.' She held a warning finger up and wagged it in Fernando's direction. 'And don't try telling me that you're his boss because that little toad, for a price, croaked who the complex does belong to and Enrique Armangual doesn't spell Fernando Serra!'

Fernando grinned widely and weighed his racket in his hands. 'But it spells the name of my cousin,' he told her rapturously.

Ruth's heart plummeted to an all-time low. 'You . . . you bastard,' she hissed angrily.

Still grinning, he challenged, 'Not a toad any more?'

Ruth shook her head in despair. 'What lengths you will go to to destroy my business,' she grated scathingly. 'I'm not even going to ask how many phone calls you made to find where I would be staying——'

'Only one,' he interjected smoothly. 'This is a very small island where information is concerned.'

'Well, you won't win because I'll find somewhere else to stay. You and your cousin don't own this island——'

'True, we don't, not all of it, but we can make things difficult for you——'

'And you are and you will,' Ruth blurted contemptuously. 'You disgust me Fernando and all this because of Maria Luisa. I thought you more of a man than that.' She turned away and was about to swing into the jeep when he strode forward and barred her way with the racket across the open doorway.

'Yes, I am more man than that and I have no intention of destroying your business. You are free to carry it on. . .when I feel fit to release you.'

'Release me?' she cried incredulously. 'Release me
from what? Eternal damnation for ever getting tied up
with you in the first place?'

'And it was a damnation, wasn't it?' Suddenly he was
deadly serious. 'For me too, Ruth. It was the worst
day's work of my life when I succumbed to your charms.
It will be interesting to see if you have lost that charm,
because you are going to need it over the next few
days, every last gram of it.'

Ruth's dark brows drew together. 'What do you
mean? What the devil are you getting at? You said
release me. . .you can't. . .' Suddenly she laughed,
forcing it out between her nervous lips. 'You . . .you're
not thinking of keeping me here?' He wasn't serious,
he couldn't be and. . .and for what?

'I'm not thinking of it any more because it is done.'

Wildly, Ruth gazed about her. Apart from the house
there were only pine trees for miles. . .and that high
stone wall. . .

She forced his tennis racket out of the way and
clambered into the jeep. This was just a wind-up, a
tease for his pleasure. He couldn't keep her here. She
started up the engine and fumbled with the gears while
he moved to the back of the vehicle and hauled out her
overnight bag.

'Keep it!' she blazed as he tossed it on to the terrace
by the front door. She found first gear and was about
to let the clutch out when suddenly he was at the door
beside her.

'You can't get out through the gates, Ruth. They
closed and locked behind you automatically. You *can*
scale the walls if you are so determined to get away,
but what then?'

'Walk!' she blazed. 'On my own two feet *if* I have to,
but I don't think that will be necessary. This sturdy
little jeep could knock six bells out of your fancy gates.'
She revved the engine threateningly.

'I don't think the car rental company would look too favourably on that, *querida*—that's if you ever managed to start it again after ramming two tons of reinforced steel.'

'It might be worth the price of a new car to get away from you!' she seethed, letting off the handbrake.

'Not worth it at all. The cost of a new one of these couldn't be offset by this contract you are working on or the next, come to that.' He reached inside the car and switched off the ignition, grinning all the time. 'Why don't you just get out of this car and come inside for a long cool drink and a long cool swim and admit defeat?'

'Defeat!' she squealed furiously. 'You haven't defeated me!'

'But I have. I have very successfully manipulated you here and I am keeping you here. That makes me the winner, you the loser; that's defeat for you in any language.'

'Manipulated me here?' Ruth cried incredulously. 'You mean. . .no, you couldn't have known I'd stoop to bribery?'

'No, that was a bonus for the receptionist,' he grinned. 'You will get your money back,' he assured her, still grinning. 'You could have got the information for nothing if you had been a little more persuasive, a little more patient. He was instructed to tell you everything you wanted to know but make you squirm a little on the way.'

'You. . .you. . . You're out of your mind! So you've got me here, very clever, but for God's sake what do you want me here for?'

No smiles now, no mockery or teasing. Only deadly serious intent. His eyes were suddenly cold and implacable. 'To make you pay, *querida*,' he told her flintily, 'to make you pay.'

After holding her gaze just long enough to finalise

the threat he turned and went towards the front door of the house, picking up her overnight bag from the terrace as he went.

Ruth was out of the car in an instant, up the steps after him.

'To pay for what?' she cried hysterically. 'For Steve? Some sort of warped vengeance for him being your mistress's previous lover?' Oh, God, but he must really love her to be able to lower himself to this. 'What do you expect to happen, Fernando? Do you hope that Steve will come looking for me and then you can string him up for making love to her before you did? Their affair was a long time ago and has nothing to do with now. You have Maria Luisa——'

'And you have your Steve back,' he accused darkly, 'and it should be enough to satisfy us all, but it isn't because sometimes affairs leave behind a tangled web of anguish. I don't suppose your partner considered for a minute what heartache he might have left behind in Seville. Maria Luisa loved him.'

Ruth's heart momentarily lifted for Steve. She supposed that Maria Luisa must have turned to Fernando in her despair when Steve had left Seville and that was how their affair had started; now Fernando was so besotted it edged towards obsession and he was doing crazy things like holding her here against her will for some sort of revenge on Steve.

'Steve called her and she never called back, probably because you had already thrust your way into her life. How dare you accuse Steve of leaving heartache behind when you were——?' Suddenly Ruth's eyes filled with tears and she took a step back. 'Let me go, Fernando,' she pleaded in a half-whisper. 'I. . . I don't want to be involved in this. Steve and Maria Luisa. . .' She shook her head dismally, her jet hair wisping across her flushed face. This was all about them and somehow she and Fernando didn't exist.

'It hurts you, does it?' he questioned unexpectedly softly.

'Yes,' she breathed awkwardly. 'Any reminders of Seville are painful.' She directed her eyes to his, secretly willing him to see the truth that had nothing to do with her partner or Maria Luisa—the truth that she had loved him then and still did. But he would never see it because his heart was more concerned with the new love of his life and some sort of retribution for the past.

'I'll make you a drink,' he said quietly, averting his eyes from hers, 'and then you can settle in.' He pushed open the arched wooden door of his house and went in, leaving Ruth standing out on the terrace.

The inviting coolness of the old stone house tempted her inside. She was desperately thirsty and perhaps over a drink Fernando would calm down enough to open the gates for her to drive out and back to Palma. She would go back there and talk to Steve and they would probably decide to abort this whole campaign and return to England. But there were clients to consider and—damnation!—there was something even more serious to consider. Supposing Steve and Maria Luisa got back together again? How would Fernando Serra react to that? Gloomily Ruth followed him.

He didn't speak as he led her through a stone-floored hallway to a sweeping staircase. Ruth pattered after him, her sandals on the polished stone the only sound.

'Fernando,' she said softly as he reached the bottom step, 'this is ridiculous. I can't stay her.'

'You can and you will,' he threw over his shoulder as he began his ascent. 'You have no choice, none at all.'

Dragging her feet, Ruth wearily went after him. Why not humour him now and reason with him later when she was feeling more refreshed? After a drink she might enjoy slamming to him the suggestion that Steve and Maria Luisa might get back together again.

Her suite of rooms was cool and restful and there was a small balcony beyond the bedroom window. Ruth sat down on the edge of the bed after he had left her, instructing her to come downstairs when she was refreshed and join him outside by the pool for a drink.

'You'll soon find your way about and settle,' were his last words after she had protested yet again that she didn't want to stay.

He was so stubborn and blind and ridiculously old-fashioned and yet weren't those attributes part of the attraction in the first place? Stubbornness she had seen as assertiveness, a strength she admired in a man. He knew what he wanted and got it. His hotel empire was proof of that. His blindness was more spiritual and endeared him to her. He seemed unaware of how attractive he was to women. His life had been spent building empires. There had been women but he had taken them almost absent-mindedly and dropped them equally absent-mindedly. Ruth had taken away his blinkers and he'd seen her love and revelled in it.

'For the good it did me,' Ruth murmured as she got up to go to the shower-room. 'I opened his eyes all right and now those eyes only see Maria Luisa.'

And his old-fashioned ways, so refreshing after today's men. He was courteous and considerate and treated her like someone so very special. And she had been special, Ruth gritted to herself as she rubbed her body liberally with shower gel. He had said so, so what the hell had happened? Why, oh, why had he let her go so easily and why, oh, why was he doing this to her now?

She dressed in what she had come in—black Bermuda shorts and a thin black cotton vest-top. Her golden tan, the gloss of her jet hair and the brightness of her blue eyes were enough to lift the sombreness of the outfit to designer chic.

Fernando had adored the way she dressed in Seville,

said she looked like a stunning sexy witch in the black
she favoured so much. . . Oh, hell, why couldn't she
stop living in the past and face this mess she was in
now?

Ruth went down the stone stairs that curved to the
ground floor and followed the archways that led to an
inner courtyard that might have been uncomfortably
hot but was tempered by a cool fountain that arced
water over a frolicking marble dolphin and child below.
Ruth gazed about her in awe. His home was beautiful,
shady and cool. There were Moorish arches everywhere
and huge earthenware pots filled with whispery green
ferns and bright geraniums and spiky yuccas. Ruth
found secret corners with grey stone seats and jasmine
scenting the air. In spite of her inner turmoil she felt
the pull of the tranquillity of the place. His Majorcan
home.

The swimming-pool area at the rear of the mellow
old house was built in keeping with the house. No
sheet of Olympic-proportion aqua-blue but a curving
arc of pale green water set in natural stone with palm-
frond umbrellas shading rustic wooden tables round the
edge.

Fernando sat at one of those tables, reading the
Diario de Mallorca newspaper as if he hadn't a care in
the world, which he hadn't, Ruth supposed, other than
considering new ways to torment her and Steve.

Ruth sat down and he looked across at her. 'That's
better; you look less flustered.' He folded his newspaper and laid it down on a seat beside him.

'I might look it but I don't feel it, Fernando. I don't
see the point of all this, keeping me here this way.'

'Relax and enjoy it.'

'I didn't come to Majorca to enjoy. I came here to
work and you are stopping me doing that.'

He leaned forward and poured her a long cool glass
of freshly squeezed orange juice. 'There are more

important things than work, Ruth,' he told her sombrely. 'I thought you might have realised that after all this time.' He raised his eyes to hers, searching, searching. 'But you obviously haven't,' he added dully.

Ruth went scarlet, looked away. Damn him, her work was important to her. He wasn't being fair and he hadn't been fair a year ago. Oh, God, but had she been fair? Why hadn't they gone into all this at the time, really thrashed it out? Now it was hopelessly too late.

'This package we are putting together *is* important. I don't want to let my clients down. You as a business-man should understand that.' She said it deliberately firmly to hide her hurt.

'I do and I'm not stopping you working, just delaying it a bit.'

'Why?'

'Because I choose to; now tell me what your lover said when he returned last night.'

Ruth drank thirstily because it was her first priority and because she was going to enjoy the next delicious moment and wanted to savour the expectancy of it. Slowly she put her glass down on the table.

'Don't you mean when he came in at *dawn*?' she breathed provocatively. As soon as she said it she realised he must know that anyway. Well, a barbed reminder could do no harm.

'Yes, it was dawn, wasn't it? So how did you feel when he slid into your bed at that hour?'

She wanted to wound him as he was wounding her so she gave him a charming smile and said, 'How did *you* feel, Fernando, when Maria Luisa slid into your bed at that hour?'

His eyes narrowed. 'This isn't funny.'

'I think it's a scream,' Ruth stated jauntily, helping herself to more juice, 'our lovers out most of the night, with each other. Hollywood would turn it down on the grounds that it held no street credibility. Fact is certainly more fascinating than fiction.'

'You really aren't taking this very seriously.'

'How can I? You are asking the most unserious questions.' She suddenly let out a long sigh and swept her hair from her face. 'I haven't spoken to Steve about all this. I left before he was awake ——'

Fernando frowned. 'So you haven't talked?'

Ruth wondered at that frown but not for long. 'Look, Fernando, I don't care what Steve and Maria Luisa were doing all night ——'

'But I do,' he interjected fiercely. 'I told you, I don't want her hurt again.'

'So why did you let her rush out of the restaurant and then let Steve follow? You could have gone after them.'

'Someone stopped me,' he reminded her.

Ruth shook her head. 'If you were really so concerned for her you wouldn't have taken any notice of me. I think you wanted them to have some time together but. . .but perhaps not most of the night,' she finished on a whisper.

She gazed at him through her thick lashes. Perhaps he thought that by giving them some space Maria Luisa would get Steve out of her system. Ruth looked away from Fernando's strained features. It hurt her to see him like this, resorting to holding her here to get revenge on Steve. It hurt her to think that Fernando cared deeply enough for another woman to do it. It wasn't like him, it was out of character, but she wasn't acting to character either. She wanted to hurt him, and how could you want to do that to someone you loved?

'You're right,' he said at last. 'I saw no point in trying to keep them apart, but I didn't expect them to spend so much time together. Maria Luisa had a lot to come to terms with ——'

'Fernando. . .' Ruth interrupted softly.

He looked across at her, warily, because of the change in her tone.

'Do. . .do you love her very much?' She wanted to know, painful though it was. She loved this man and she knew more than he did at the moment. She knew that Steve adored Maria Luisa and that there was a good chance of them getting together again, and if they did only one person would suffer and that would be Fernando. The need to hurt him drained out of her as she waited for his answer.

'I believe I've already answered that question,' he said at last. 'Now let me ask you one. Do you love Steve very much?'

Ruth couldn't let this go on. 'Fernando,' she husked, 'I care very deeply for Steve ——'

'And you love him.'

'No, I don't love him, not the way you mean.'

'But you live with him, you make love with him ——'

'I do not!' Ruth cried. 'This has got to stop, Fernando. Steve and I have a very good business relationship. We work well together and we are really good friends. . .'

Fernando's eyes narrowed at that and his finely defined lips thinned. Ruth sighed.

'Yes, I know that sounds clichéd but it's the truth. There is nothing sexual between us. Can't you understand that men and women can have that sort of relationship?'

'No,' he said bluntly, coiling his fingers together in his lap. 'I can't see it. Perhaps if I didn't know you so intimately I could be convinced, but I know your sexuality and your demands ——'

'Will you stop that?' she blazed hotly. 'You make me sound like some crazed nymphomaniac. I was engaged to be married once, an engagement that was a mistake and I was lucky to get out of without too much trouble and then I met you and that is the sum total of my "sexual demands" as you put it. I don't sleep with Steve; I didn't before Seville or after and I never will. Does that satisfy you?'

'Not in the least,' he returned coldly. 'I don't believe you. You didn't deny all this last night, so why now?'

'It suited me not to deny it last night,' Ruth blurted and stared beyond him to a young palm swaying gently in the breeze. She heard cicadas thrumming in the olive trees and her stomach wrenched because of the memories that sound conjured up.

'To what end?'

She turned her head slightly to look him in the face. This would take some courage but something inside her was urging her to be honest. Her fingers in her lap intertwined to power her strength.

'Last night I wanted you to be jealous,' she told him bluntly. 'You accused me of having a lover and I chose not to deny it.'

He smiled wryly. 'You chose not to deny it because I had Maria Luisa on my arm. Now she isn't here and you are denying it. I wonder what you think to gain by that?'

'Certainly not your undying love and affection,' Ruth stated frostily. 'Don't forget, I don't *choose* to be here now. If you had left well alone and let me carry on my business I wouldn't be here. I'm denying my supposed affair now because I'm fed up with your accusations. They're pointless anyway. You don't care what I'm up to; your only concern is for Maria Luisa's feelings.'

'I don't suppose it ever occurred to you that I was jealous when I saw you with him last night?' he said softly.

His eyes weren't even on her when he said that, and Ruth couldn't take it seriously.

'Not for a second. You knew who Steve was—my business partner.'

'I recognised him from Seville, yes.'

'You didn't accuse me of having an affair with him then, so why now?'

He did look at her then, very directly, very unemotionally. 'Because last year I was crazy about you, blind to everyone and everything,' he said quietly.

It was all he said and somehow it was enough for Ruth. He'd loved her then but not now. Well, she knew that already but it didn't balm the pain.

'And this year you're crazy about Maria Luisa,' Ruth murmured, gazing down at the fingers she had been wringing till they were red and hot. She let out a ragged sigh of resignation and wiped her hands down her shorts. 'I don't understand you, Fernando. Here we are, two ex-lovers, talking about another pair of ex-lovers, and what the hell has it to do with us and what the hell do you hope to gain by keeping me here? Steve won't come for me, you know.'

'I don't expect him to,' Fernando said solemnly. 'That wasn't the point of all this. I have no wish to see him again. I just hope that you issued him with that warning because I meant what I said—I'll ruin him if he hurts her again.'

Ruth frowned. 'I really don't understand you. I thought all this was to get back at Steve for his having had an affair with Maria Luisa.'

'Yes, you thought and you thought wrongly. I told you why I want you here and that is to make you pay.' Slowly he got to his feet and picked up the newspaper. He rolled it and gently thudded it against his thigh.

'For what? I've done nothing,' she protested. 'I'm not sleeping with my partner. I have nothing to do with Maria Luisa's being hurt. This isn't my problem at all, it's yours!'

'Yes, it's my problem and you are the solution, *querida*.'

'Stop it, Fernando.' Ruth shot to her feet and faced him across the table. 'You are so obsessed with this

Maria Luisa you're not thinking straight. Reason it out; if you let me go I'll go straight back to Palma. Maria Luisa and Steve might even be together as we are talking. If I go back I can reason with Steve to leave her alone——'

'But not for me, for yourself because you want Steve for yourself——'

'No!' Ruth cried, clenching her fists at her sides. Oh, why couldn't he believe her? 'I don't want Steve, I never have. . . It's you. . . Her voice cracked. She couldn't say it—that he was the only one she wanted. 'It's. . .it's you who's being so unreasonable,' she stammered.

'I think I am being very reasonable, and let me make one thing quite clear. I am not trying to punish you for what Steve did to Maria Luisa. Soon he will have his own conscience to live with and that is punishment for any man.' He moved around the table to her and as he moved he spoke slowly and meaningfully. 'You are right, this has nothing to do with them, this is between you and me. Fernando and Ruth, Ruth and Fernando.' His free hand came up to grasp her chin and twist her face towards him. His eyes were jet, his jawline hard and chiselled. 'Don't look so alarmed. I'm not a violent man. I won't use force because I won't need to. I don't even believe you are aware of your crime.' His thumb grazed over her jawline as he serached her eyes. 'But you committed one, Ruth, and one you will pay for. How many times did I tell you I loved you back in Seville?'

Ruth shook her head, tried to twist it out of his menacing grasp. She was afraid now, afraid for her life and her future.

'Enough times to sound convincing by my standards,' he grated, answering his own question. 'But no more, *querida*; I've paid and now you will pay.'

'Don't threaten me,' she managed to seethe through her clenched teeth.

'But I will, because I enjoy it,' he told her forcefully. Then his thumb moved to her lips and scored them brutally and then he jerked her away from him.

Ruth's eyes were wide with emotional pain. 'What on earth has happened to you?' she breathed. 'You've changed. You're like some bitter clone of the Fernando I once knew.'

He smiled. 'And who was that Fernando? This one maybe.'

He lifted his hand and she flinched because she thought he was going to strike her, but it was worse. His hand slid the vest-top from one shoulder and his hand immediately smoothed over her golden flesh. The caress on her warm skin whirlpooled her emotions till she nearly drowned in her own liquid senses. The sensation was immediate, fire on her soul, a fiery punishment for the love she had allowed.

'Don't—don't do that.' Her small white teeth drew in her upper lip as his hand stroked so erotically, his thumb tracing circles of white heat.

'What does it make you think of? Our first time, the afternoon we couldn't keep our hands and our mouths away from each other. The time we discovered what true eroticism tasted like, the time you cried when I entered you, cried for more——'

'You bastard!'

'Yes, so you keep telling me. You'll believe it by the time you leave here——'

'I believe it now, Fernando,' Ruth spat. 'I understand what you're doing now.' She jerked her shoulder out of his reach and furiously pulled her top back into position. She wasn't sure, though. It seemed too incredible. 'You think by keeping me here you can drive me wild with need.' She smiled. 'You probably can and you probably will and probably the inevitable will happen and this. . .this will be a repeat of Seville. And then what, Fernando?'

She tried to act flippant by shrugging her shoulders and holding out her palms but inside she felt far from flippant. She hurt so much it was physical pain, like a knife twisting backwards and forwards.

'It won't get as far as "then what", Ruth. In fact it will get nowhere. You seem to be under the misapprehension that I intend making love to you.' He shook his dark head. 'No chance, *querida*. I have the memories of the last time we loved to carry me through to my grave. I don't want your body, the heat of your kisses, your secret self closing around my passion, your liquid fire pulsing against mine. I've had all that and lived to tell the tale. All I want out of life is some good old-fashioned revenge for a good old-fashioned love-affair that went wrong. And I was very old-fashioned, wasn't I? I actually believed you were in love with me, and all you were out for was a good time.'

Ruth's heart recoiled painfully from that. Hadn't she thought the very same thing—that he had used her, that it was just one of those flings? But she was too hurt to argue, too stricken with pain to reason with him. She went to turn away but he caught her. The paper slid from his hands and he grasped her firmly by her shoulders.

'I pleaded with you to stay but you turned your back on me for your career and your partner. You used me in Seville and you haven't even the decency to deny it—for me or your own self-respect.'

Almost numb with shock, Ruth struggled to fight back. 'I left my respect back in Seville where you left your sensibility, Fernando. So you want to punish me, do you? Try it. You might reveal more of your own frailties than mine, and then who will be punishing whom will be very interesting to behold.'

He let her go and smiled cruelly. 'I like a challenge. I rise to it, but don't get too excited by that,' he stated suggestively, 'because that is the only thing I intend to rise to. I won't make love to you ever again and that is giving you a fighting chance because now you know the outcome in advance. But I promise you that I'll have some fun on the way. I want to see you on your knees begging for my love before our time is up, and that will be all the satisfaction I need.'

He turned and strode away from her, leaving her weak and sickened and just a little afraid. She bit her lip and knew that she deserved such punishment. She had made a wrong choice a year ago, had put Steve and her career before the man she loved, but there had been more to it than that. She had contrarily thought that if he really cared he would have come running after her. Where on earth had she got her muddled values from? She wanted a career and a love and both were possible so why hadn't she called him, written to him? These days women were allowed to take up the running, but she hadn't and now it was too late. But hell, why was she taking all the blame and why was she letting him punish her when he could easily have done some of the running himself? Well, damn him, she wasn't going to be put down, she just wasn't!

Slowly Ruth peeled off her vest-top and wriggled out of her shorts. There was no one around so, naked, she stepped towards the pool-edge and braced herself, drawing deep breaths into her lungs. She raised her arms, stretched her long tanned body in the heat of the sun. She felt desire and arousal as a warm breeze rippled over her breasts. She felt an aching need for Fernando to soothe away the pain of desire from her loins. She wanted him but couldn't have him and she *must* deal with that because he had forewarned her.

Silly man, she thought as she dived head first into the calming cool water that drove all desire from her body in a single shuddering thrust. Silly, silly man, she mused as she struck out strongly for the other side of the pool. He's underestimated my strength.

CHAPTER FIVE

RUTH unpacked the few clothes she had brought with her and hung them up in the wardrobe in the dressing-room then she plugged in her hairdrier and blow-dried her hair in front of the dressing-table mirror.

After her swim she had sprawled in the hot sun to dry off naturally then dressed and lazily explored the lovely Mediterranean gardens. There were dwarf fan palms where lazy lizards sought shade from the hot sun and thick-leaved aloes which Ruth skirted with care — the points were like needles. Heliotropes sweetly scented the air and were covered with tiny bees gathering pollen. She had found the tennis courts and the machine that served up a constant succession of tennis balls. So Fernando had been playing by himself — her heart bled for him! She'd found no sign of life anywhere on her travels, no supporting staff, though the house and gardens looked as if an army of faithful family retainers had slaved there for centuries.

She wondered which part of the house Fernando and Maria Luisa occupied, which were their own personal quarters, because so far she had seen nothing that indicated that a happy couple occupied the place.

After drying her hair Ruth tied it back from her face with a white velvet ribbon and planned her next move. She had no intention of fighting for her freedom any more. She'd phone Steve later and find out what he was doing and then she would use any information she had about him and Maria Luisa to irritate her way out of the Casa Pinar. Fernando Serra would wish he'd never started this.

'I am free to make some phone calls, am I? I promise

faithfully not to call the police or the British consul or Interpol. I just want to phone Steve and find out what he and Maria Luisa were doing all night — as if I can't guess.'

She'd found him showered and changed into light-weight jeans and a white polo shirt and reading in the shade of the cloister-like gallery terrace that ran along the back of the house overlooking the gardens and the pool. He pulled a wicker chair into the shade for her.

Ruth pushed it back into the full glare of the sun and slumped down into it, raising her face to the hot sun to absorb its rays.

'Yes, of course you're free to use the phone,' he told her lazily, 'and free to call who you like, including the police or whoever — with one exception, that is. You can't call your partner.'

Ruth didn't move, not a muscle other than the ones to widen her lips into a grin. 'Oh, really?' she uttered smugly as if it didn't matter at all. 'You do sleep at some time, I presume?' she asked rhetorically. 'I'll make my calls then.'

'Tea?'

Ruth blinked open her eyes and stared at him. He was unruffled, pouring tea from a beautiful silver teapot into white bone-china cups. He handed her a plate of freshly baked *ensaimadas* from a tray set out on a white linen cloth. Ruth took a plate from the tray and took two of the spiral flaky-pastry cakes. She'd had no lunch and was beginning to feel the effects of not eating for so long.

'So you have a housekeeper?'

He frowned as he handed her a cup of tea. Ruth took it and nodded to the table. 'All that — it looks beautiful. I wandered around after my swim but didn't see any staff. Where do you keep them, down in the dungeons ball-chained to the wall and only released for your pleasures?'

He smiled, untouched by her sarcasm. 'I have a full staff here but I released them for the fiesta in Palma. Kind and considerate, aren't I?'

'Very; you'll be telling me next you baked these yourself.' She bit into the flaky whirls and smothered a moan of pleasure. They were so good.

'I did but I cheated—cooked them from frozen, but tonight I promise to cook you a proper meal, my own personal favourite. A delicious *escaladun*—chicken stew in English.'

'What are you trying to do, kill me with kindness?'

'You are my guest——'

'Your prisoner.'

She munched her pastries and drank her tea and felt better for it, stronger, sharper, ready for battle.

'I will phone Steve, you know, whether you like it or not,' she declared determinedly.

'It's not a case of whether I like it or not, more a case of whether you can find him or not.'

Ruth's stomach tightened. Surely Steve hadn't done a runner? She could see it all—Fernando's heavies hauling Steve from his bed this morning, threatening him with concrete trainers and a long drop into the sea from Fernando's yacht. . . Ruth leaned forward and took another *ensaimada*; she was still so hungry it was definitely affecting her brain.

'Where is he?' she asked between mouthfuls.

'He left the apartment this morning——'

'My God, you didn't pay him off, you didn't bribe him to leave Maria Luisa alone?' she cried in despair.

Fernando refilled her teacup, letting out a sigh of disbelief as he did it.

'Well, I don't know, do I?' she protested. 'You've done some very funny things lately; I wouldn't put anything beyond you.'

'And you obviously wouldn't put accepting a bribe beyond you partner either, would you?'

'I didn't mean it to sound that way,' Ruth huffed. 'Of course he wouldn't take a bribe from you, or anyone, come to that, and especially someone trying to bribe him out of the country because of a woman—one he happens to love very much.'

She expected to see signs of fury in his eyes at that stab but she saw nothing to indicate any such irritation.

'Did you hear me? she urged, dying for him to get cross.

He smiled and nodded. 'Yes, I heard, and feeble you sound too, or is the word pathetic?'

Probably both, Ruth thought to herself. Trying to wind him up wasn't proving very successful.

'He's probably out working,' she suggested. 'I'll ring him later. How come you know he's not in anyway?'

He made her wait for an answer as he topped the teapot up with hot water and Ruth's imagination went off on its own. Steve would have read her note, waited for her to phone and say she had arrived safely and when she hadn't he would have driven up to the north of the island to find her. Poor Steve, he'd be going frantic by now.

'He's spending a few days with Maria Luisa in Valencia on the mainland,' Fernando told her at last.

Ruth nearly choked on the last crumb of her pastry. She swallowed her tea to clear her throat. 'In Valencia with Maria Luisa?' she croaked.

'She told me this morning when she got back to the yacht that they planned on going. She phoned half an hour ago to say they were on their way.'

Ruth felt her insides burning up. 'And. . .and you let her go? You approve of her flying off with her ex-lover?' Ruth let out an explosive sound of disbelief. 'You, Fernando Serra, are either lying through your teeth, putting on a brave face or you have the same loose sort of arrangement with your mistress as you accused me of having with Steve.'

'Or I have supreme confidence in myself that she will return to me,' he told her smoothly.

Somehow Ruth felt betrayed in more ways than one. Fernando wasn't the proud man she'd thought he was and Steve was a creep to have just gone off without letting her know why, with whom and for how long. Damn him, he might have told her.

'I wouldn't be so sure of that,' Ruth stated tartly, 'They were once lovers, don't forget.'

'How can I forget? But I am still nevertheless certain she will return to me, because I have something very precious that Steve Cannock hasn't got.'

'Don't tell me,' Ruth seethed. 'I can well imagine what it is.'

'Yes, with your mind I expect you can,' he teased.

This wasn't how it was meant to be. He was the one supposed to be feeling threatened.

'You've changed since last night,' Ruth told him in a soft murmur. 'Last night you were threatening to ruin him if he hurt Maria Luisa again; now you're condoning their going away together.'

Fernando began to stack the dirty cups and saucers on the tray. 'Today I am confident that he can't hurt her any more. Maria Luisa isn't the gullible little girl she was last year in Seville. She has become a mature, sensible woman.'

'All credit to you, no doubt!'

He nodded. 'Yes, I could take the credit and I will. So who can take the *discredit* for the change in you this last year?'

Ruth looked at him in puzzlement. 'I haven't changed,' she retorted.

'Oh, but you have. Last year you were open and natural, loving and thoughtful—until you left me, that is. Now you have a bitter streak I've never seen before.'

Ruth shook her head and smiled in disbelief. 'If I'm bitter it's because I resent being here. I resent you for engineering it and I resent you for what you think you can do to me in revenge for our affair last year.'

'And is that how you show your resentment, by stripping off naked in front of me and rippling your sexy body invitingly?'

His dancing dark eyes voyaged up and down her seated form as if reminding himself.

Colour swamped Ruth's face and she turned away. 'I didn't know you were watching,' she huffed irritably.

'Like hell you didn't,' Fernando snorted. 'It was a good performance, plotted and delivered with artistry and skill and aimed at an audience. It worked too, turned me on as much as it turned you on, but don't get too smart——'

She turned her face back to him. 'Why, because you might not be able to control that white-hot passion of yours while your mistress is away? You sicken me. That's why I'm here, isn't it? It's more than just revenge. You *do* intend to make love to me while Maria Luisa is away. It's why you aren't unduly worried that she's away with Steve. You know Steve and better the devil you know than the one you don't——'

'And while the cat is away the mouse will play——'

'Shut up, Fernando!' Ruth cried hotly. 'This is damned serious.'

'Is it now? You obviously think so and that indicates what I had suspected all along—that you really are upset at the thought of your lover being away with Maria Luisa; hence your ridiculous outcries and accusations.'

'He is *not* my lover,' Ruth stated emphatically, 'but yes, I am upset at the thought of him spending time with Maria Luisa. Because I care about him and last year he got terribly hurt and I wouldn't want it to happen again. So far all I've heard from you is bleating about Maria Luisa's feelings; well, I care about Steve's——'

'And here we two are,' Fernando said on a sigh, 'wasting breath over two adults who are quite capable of looking after themselves.'

'And *enjoying* themselves,' she added pointedly.

'You can't hurt me, Ruth,' he said calmly, 'so stop trying to. I'm dealing with my feelings about those two in a sensible adult way——'

'By condoning it?' Ruth husked. 'Very *now*-thinking but very out of character for you. You used to be such a sweet old-fashioned thing last year,' she simpered sarcastically.

'Till I met you.' He stood up, stretched and bent to pick up the tray. 'Come on, I'll show you where the kitchen is.'

Ruth tucked herself further down in the wicker chair and hoisted up her cotton skirt to expose her long legs to the heat of the sun. 'No, thanks. I'm no substitute for an absent servant——'

'Nor an absent lover,' he grated, 'so put yourself away. Your sexuality is wasted on me.'

Ruth was still fuming long after he'd gone. She was hot too, too hot to sunbathe. She went back to her room, pulled the wooden shutters across the windows and lay on the bed. She was asleep in three seconds flat.

'In spite of no one being here but you and me I shall dress for dinner tonight, and expect you to do likewise.'

Ruth blinked open her eyes, not sure where she was. The room was dim till Fernando crossed the bedroom and opened the shutters.

She stretched but didn't feel a lot better for her siesta. 'Don't walk into my bedroom without knocking again,' she instructed on a yawn.

'I did, you didn't answer. I thought you were dead.'

Ruth slid her feet to the floor. 'You normally chat up corpses, do you?'

'What's "chat up"?'

He came back to the bedside and picked up an already opened bottle of red wine from the bedside table. Ruth looked up at him with pain in her heart as he poured two glasses. In Seville he had often pleaded ignorance over some of the expressions she used. It was a game they played. His spoken English was perfect, as was his comprehension, the result of a few years at Oxford studying languages—four in all.

Ruth leaned back and coiled her legs under her and took the glass of wine he offered. 'Thanks—just like old times, what?'

'Does your flippancy conceal a regret that those old times are gone forever?' He sat a foot away from her on the edge of the bed.

'And they are gone forever,' she mumbled after taking a sip of wine.

'Do you regret what happened to us in Seville?' he asked levelly.

Ruth stared down into her wine and spoke softly. 'What did happen to us in Seville, Fernando?' She raised her eyes to look into his. Perhaps now she might get an idea of what went wrong.

His eyes were unreadable but a small pulse at the edge of his lips was preparing for a dismissive smile. 'I'm not sure now. Then I was. I thought I was in love. I thought you were in love. I thought we loved each other.' He lowered his eyes and the smile never happened. 'But here we are, drinking wine sitting on a bed that in former times would have been on fire by now.'

Ruth couldn't help a smile. 'Yes,' she murmured, and then, because it was all too painful, she muttured, 'Did you say something about dressing for dinner when you woke me up.'

'We generally do.'

'You and Maria Luisa?' She was making it worse for

herself but couldn't help it. Like watching him on his yacht with her last night, agonising but compulsive.

'Yes, when we are here.'

'Aren't you always here?'

'No, we spread our time between here, Palma, the yacht and the villa in Valencia.'

'Don't you ever work?' she asked ruefully.

He nodded. 'Of course, but I delegate a lot now.'

Ruth was surprised. 'You didn't use to. I always had the impression you were a workaholic.'

'I was hardly a workaholic when we were together in Seville.' He grinned suddenly. 'More a bedaholic.'

She grinned with him. 'Did I change you?' she asked daringly.

He seemed to consider that for a few seconds and then replied, 'Maria Luisa needed me around.'

Would it never end, the punishment and the pain? For a minute she had believed she might have been responsible for the change in his life, but it wasn't her but Maria Luisa. Some power she must hold over him.

'This. . .this villa in Valencia, is it where. . .where she and Steve have gone?'

'Could be,' he said evasively.

'I wasn't trying to find out where they are,' Ruth said quickly. 'I'm just. . .well. . .still surprised you are taking this so coolly.'

He didn't respond to that and Ruth sipped more wine. 'Did. . .did you. . .were you having an affair with her before Seville?' She clutched her wine glass fiercely. Why was she doing this, hurting herself so badly?

'Like you and Steve?'

She rolled her eyes in sufferance. 'You know we weren't, Fernando. Do you think I could have been as I was with you if I was already heavily involved with someone else?'

'Yet you question me,' he said quietly.

There were deep shadows across the room now and

his face was in one of them so she couldn't see his ey
clearly. She wanted to see his eyes because they mi
rored his moods. She felt a change now, as if he was
beginning to feel sorry for himself. She didn't understand that, not at all. He couldn't have any regrets. He
had everything to live for and someone to share his life.
That void called 'a future without him' loomed ever-
larger.

'It's different,' she smoothed. 'You and Maria Luisa
are living together now and it suggests you were
involved before.'

'It suggests nothing of the sort but as it happens you
are partly right. We knew each other before the Expo,
though not quite so intimately as now.' He refilled the
glasses.

'So how did it happen? You and Maria Luisa?'

She really wanted to know; though it would be
painful, she knew it was the only way. It was somehow
better than making her own suppositions, which seemed
to take an awful amount of energy and caused a lot of
stress. Perhaps when she knew every last detail of their
affair she could blank it all out and start all over again
. . .and the dawn might never come!

'We needed each other,' he clipped and got up. 'As I
was saying, we usually dress for dinner——'

'Well, we can't ruin an age-old custom for the sake
of an absent mistress, can we?' she interrupted as she
untwined her legs and stood up to face him. Pain and
jealousy had spurred that sarcastic retort. 'I'm afraid a
very weathered cotton sundress is the best I can
muster——'

'That will do nicely,' he said tightly, gathering up the
wine bottle and glasses. 'And the other age-old custom
is a romantic walk before dinner, to take in the sunset.
I hope you'll join me?'

Such cruelty. She had the feeling he was winning. 'I
don't think so——'

'I do. Read insist for hope,' he suggested drily.

Oh, no, he wasn't going to get it all his own way. She smiled sweetly. 'Oh, you should have said. That throws a whole new light on it. Your word is my command,' she whined sarcastically, and then the smile evaporated and her eyes narrowed coldly. 'You walk alone, Fernando, because I don't trot submissively in absent mistresses' footsteps!'

The glasses and the bottle of wine were slammed back down on the bedside table and then his hand around her wrist was a shock. With just a small tug she was off balance and pulled against him. His cheek brushed hers with a cathartic effect on her senses. They all reared and exploded inside her — touch, smell, taste. It all came back, Seville and its magic. His erotic caresses, his musky masculinity warmed with the scent of his cologne. She forced hatred to her soul, for him and for the unwanted desire that leapt unbidden to her pulses at the taste of his mouth on hers. Her heart spun as his lips closed over hers, spun and raged and thundered inside her.

She had dreamt of this moment, fantasised it in her mind so many lonely dark nights, and now it was happening and nothing had prepared her for this self-destruction. In spite of his cruelty and his love for Maria Luisa, the desire and the need for him were still there.

His arms tightened around her, urging her fiercely against him, and her whole body became treacherously suppliant. She had no control, none whatsoever. She clung to him, like a weak, mad thing lost in the catacombs of hell and finding a soul to clutch at.

His tongue parted her lips sensuously and then he drew so hard on her mouth that her last vestige of hope disappeared. She wanted him more than ever, loved him more than ever. The kiss deepened, driving her hard down into total despair. This was a game to him, a game of revenge. . .

The delicate tracing of his fingers over her naked breast nearly clouded her mind off forever. With a sob she drew her mouth from his and cried out as she threw her head back. Her teeth bit hard into her lower lip. She heard his deep, shuddering breath at her breast and then his mouth encompassed her raging nipple, drawing ravenously on it.

She wanted the strength to be the first to pull away but it wouldn't come, that little bit extra that would separate desire from decency.

And then suddenly it was there, the resolve not to be used and hurt. It coincided with his drawing back from her so that it appeared he was the one to call a halt first.

She was shaking as she lurched back, almost as if he had thrust her away from him. Feverishly she adjusted her top over her burning breasts.

'A challenge?' she husked painfully, her eyes so wide she thought he must surely read the anguish in them.

He was completely in control. Cold, hard and resolute. His voice reflected that as he spoke. 'How can it be a challenge when we both know the outcome?'

Ruth shook her head. 'You might know it but I don't.' She clawed her hair from her hot forehead. 'I don't believe for a minute that you have no intention of making love to me. We were lovers once, Fernando,' she went on hotly. 'You can't just switch your emotions on and off like a light-switch.'

'You did, after Seville,' he said coldly. He brought his hand up to her eye level and snapped his fingers. 'Just like that, Ruth. You snapped it off just like that.'

Ruth bit her lip and stared at him, not knowing what to say or do. He believed that and she believed the same of him, and now. . .? And now it was horribly too late to do anything about it. Maria Luisa had the place in his heart that was once hers. Oh, God, how ridiculous all this was. They had had so much in Seville and now this bitterness, hatred, mistrust. Everything that was ugly and nothing that was beautiful.

He switched the subject just as he had snapped his fingers to remind her of how she had switched off after Seville. 'That walk. I insist you take it with me.'

The strength was there now, a little late but there nevertheless. She lifted her chin to show that strength and her defiance. 'Yes, I will,' she conceded politely, 'because it will show you can't hurt me. I'm immune to pain,' she lied. 'Throw what you will at me but it won't make any difference. Yes, I'll come on that romantic stroll with you and watch the sunset as we did in Seville and I'll remind you of it, just as you intend to remind me of it, and I'll go with you all of the cruel way, Fernando, and when it's all over I hope it gives you the satisfaction you crave.'

She lifted the bottle and glasses and slammed them at him. 'Now get out and leave me to get ready in peace.'

Without a word he left her and it was his failure to make a suitable response that really got to her. She had wanted him to slam something back at her, a denial, an agreement, another challenge, anything but that infuriating silence.

A huge sob caught in her throat as she rushed across the room to slam the door after him.

A clutch of sweet-scented jasmine twined in her hair on one side of her head uplifted and upgraded her sundress. She'd gathered the fragrant blooms from a tub outside on the narrow balcony and deeply inhaled its sweet perfume before deciding to wear it in her hair. The jasmine had been out in Seville the year before. . . she hoped he'd remember.

The apricot cotton dress was purely day wear, quite

simply cut with a straight neck and very short sleeves
and fairly short skirt. High heels would have elevated it
to borderline evening wear but she hadn't brought heels
with her so she decided on gold leather flip-flops. She
looked sassy, she thought, as she swung her long jet
hair, careful not to dislodge the jasmine. And with
lipstick and mascara and a spray of perfume she looked
damned well sexy! Hardly how she wanted to appear
when she'd planned on wearing the dress to visit the
hotels she wanted to do business with. But tonight she
wasn't working, she was warring.

She kneaded her forehead as she made her way
downstairs. She really ought to be thinking of work
instead of calling Fernando Serra's bluff. But Steve had
gone off with Maria Luisa for a few days and he wasn't
thinking about work, that was for sure, and she hadn't
her freedom anyway!

Heavens, what was going to happen to those two?
Would Steve win Maria Luisa over? For her to have
gone off with him like that showed she must still care
for him and yet she had been looking so adoringly at
Fernando on the yacht. Lucky girl, Ruth thought miserably as she followed her nose to the kitchen, a choice
of two men.

She came to the dining-room first, a vast, almost
medieval room with heavy furniture set on terracotta
floor tiles. The room was cool, so cool she shivered.
There was no table set and she looked round for a
sideboard that must house such things as cutlery.

'I've set the table outside on the terrace,' Fernando
told her, stepping through from the kitchen beyond. It
was uncanny how he often knew what she was thinking.

'So many terraces,' she mooned, refusing to acknow-
edge how amazing he looked in black trousers and a
white evening jacket; even the tea-towel over his
shoulder did nothing to disarm his incredible elegance.

'Same terrace, different end. You look lovely,' he

said, turning away, back into the kitchen. 'You'd look lovelier if that jasmine were in your hair and not hanging off your shoulder like that.'

Angrily she snatched at the home-made corsage. Her hair was too silky to hold flowers in it. What a dope she must have looked with it dripping over her shoulder.

'It was supposed to be in my hair,' she told him as she followed him through to the spacious kitchen, deciding honesty was the best policy in the circumstances. 'It was supposed to remind you of Seville. It was supposed to drive you wild with desire.'

'Instead it made me laugh,' he said, pushing a bowl of freshly prepared salad into the fridge, 'I hope that isn't an omen for the rest of the evening. I'd rather planned on going to bed tonight aching with the satisfaction of revenge, not laughter.'

'You'll probably go to bed with an ache somewhere else if all my plans come to fruition,' she told him insolently.

He laughed again, obviously in a good humour for the night.

'I remember when I first set eyes on you at that cocktail party and I thought, In spite of her dark flowing hair and her Mediterranean beauty she has a bite about her that can only be British. I was right, British women are continents away from any other. No Spanish woman would make such a crude remark, unless she was a gypsy woman, of course.'

Ruth raised an insolent brow to match her mood. 'No doubt why you honed in on me that night.'

'I honed in on you because you were the most beautiful creature I'd ever seen.'

Ruth smiled as he swept the tea-towel from his shoulder, flung it down and came towards her. 'And flattery will get you *anywhere* tonight,' she retorted as sexily as she could. She opened her arms as if to gather him into them but he simply grinned and walked straight past her.

'Come,' he ordered with a smile in his voice, 'follow me. I'm not ready for "anywhere" yet. Have you forgotten the ritual? How I like to do things in the old-fashioned way?'

He proceeded to remind her verbally as she followed him sheepishly out through the dining-room to a wide archway that led to the terrace, though she didn't need this painful reminder of the way they'd given in to their wild passion every evening in Seville. How could she ever forget it?

'Sunset in the Mediterranean way with fire and passion and going out in a blaze of glory,' he teased, grabbing at a blanket from the back of one of the wicker chairs on the terrace. 'Followed by making love with fire and passion and going out in a blaze of glory—*anywhere*!' he added with a laugh of pure cynicism.

CHAPTER SIX

'WHAT'S the blanket for?' Ruth asked as they strolled through the formal gardens towards a flight of stone steps that led up to a forest of dense green pine trees offering shade and coolness. 'Or is that rather a naïve question?'

He walked with one hand in his trouser pocket and the other grasping the blanket over his shoulder.

'You know me, Ruth, I like to do things in comfort.'

'And making love on a blanket in a pine forest is comfort, is it?'

'I mentioned making love as a reminder, not an intention,' he told her.

'Oh, I forgot,' she murmured, 'your resolution *not* to do it but just have some fun on the *way* to not doing it. A roll on the blanket but not in the proverbial hay.'

He laughed. 'Actually, I don't want to ruin my jacket.'

Ruth smiled. 'No consideration for my dress?'

'You did say it was weathered.'

'Yes, I did, didn't I?'

From the top of the steps a narrow worn path led through the pine forest. Ruth deeply inhaled the scent of the pines so richly sweet, warm and Mediterranean. To one side of the pines were ancient olive trees bent by the winds and cicadas buzzed non-stop in the hot night air. The forest thinned to a plateau of wind-worn scrubland and there was the aromatic scent of rosemary and thyme. For the first time Ruth saw the sea.

She cried out with pleasure. 'I had no idea the sea was so close. I lost all sense of direction getting here.'

She sighed ecstatically as they reached the cliff-top

and a warm breeze caught her hair and whirled it high above her head. The view was unbelievable. The cliff was sheer, dropping down to secret rocky coves below them with the sea gently lapping white sand. The water was dark blue but in places dark green where underwater rock formations subtly changed the colour. The sky was all around them, orange and crimson, passionate and dangerous.

'It's beautiful, Fernando! Spectacular!' She gazed in awe at it all before turning to him. 'I didn't know you had your home on this part of the island. I thought you were based in Palma.'

'I was,' he told her, snatching the blanket from his shoulder and spreading it on the ground. 'I moved here after the Expo last year.'

'Has that any special significance?' she asked bravely as she crumpled down on to the blanket and gazed up at him.

'Yes. I wanted solitude.' He squatted down beside her and plucked a piece of wild lavender and proceeded to tear it apart, little by little. He gazed out to sea and the horizon as he did it, offering no more yet giving so much away.

The sun was preparing to go out with a fury, blazing the clouds crimson and gold and firing the sea purple. Ruth divided her attention between the changing colours of the sea and sky and the profile of Fernando's head. He looked so desperately far away from her that she nearly reached out to touch him, to bring him back, because she instinctively knew where he was.

The pity of it all, she mused sadly and lay back on the rug and blinked up at the darkening sky above her. If only she could shut these eyes and open them on the past and try again.

'You soon filled that solitude,' she uttered softly. That was where a lot of the hurt lay. It was painful enough knowing they had both let their love for each

other slip so easily away, but the speed with which he'd
filled the void she'd left really cut into her. Love on the
rebound? She supposed some men were prone to it, but
surely not Fernando?

She felt him lie down beside her. She turned her head
to look at him. He leaned up on one elbow to gaze
down at her and instead of Ruth feeling a rush of panic
she felt incredibly calm.

'Maria Luisa wanted to be out of the capital,' he told
her. 'She said it stifled her.'

Ruth smiled inwardly. So she and Maria Luisa had
something else in common besides the same taste in
men. She thought that she would probably like her very
much if she met her properly. She had looked lovely at
their brief meeting in the restaurant but when Fernando
had suggested they eat together her hurt and vulner-
ability had broken through. Hardly the actions of a
mature, sensible woman, more the gullible little girl of
Seville Fernando had described. A thought suddenly
occurred to her.

'Fernando, does Maria Luisa know about you and
me?'

He laughed. 'You mean does she know we are here
together now?'

'No, actually I didn't mean that but you can answer
it anyway.'

'I suppose she does,' he told her vaguely. 'But don't
start getting any ideas that she might throw a fit of
jealousy. She's with her ex-lover too, don't forget.'

'Yes, what a tangled web,' Ruth murmured desolately. 'What I really wanted to know was why she ran
out of the restaurant. Was it because she knew we'd
had an affair and was jealous or was it the heartbreak
of coming face to face with Steve?'

'Does it matter?'

No, it didn't. Nothing really mattered any more.

'I was just curious,' she said. 'Is she from Majorca?'

Ruth asked, surprised she was handling this so well. It was the only sensible way really, to act as if they were old friends and not old lovers. Later, in the privacy of her bedroom she could gnash her teeth and let the anguish flood out.

'No, the mainland. Madrid. Her father is in the government, her mother a great campaigner for under-privileged children. Very respectable, upper-class Spanish family. They were both very distressed when she chose a career on the airlines.' Fernando smiled and shook his head. 'You British think you have the monopoly on class structure. . .their only daughter a mere air hostess. . .it didn't bear thinking about. But Maria Luisa was determined to fly.' He sighed. 'I'm sorry, you must have heard all this about Maria Luisa from your partner.'

Ruth shook her head and hooked her arm behind her neck. 'Neither of us ever spoke of Seville after that trip. Not the personal side of it.' She half smiled in the last threads of gold that smouldered in the sky. 'Believe it or not, the first time we spoke of our affairs was last night in the restaurant. I saw you and Maria Luisa on your yacht. Steve couldn't see: he had his back to you. I recognised her but I didn't know how Steve would take it if he saw you together. I went a little crazy and started gabbling on about you and love and him and Maria Luisa. I just wanted to know how deep his feelings for her were.'

'It sounds as if you were more concerned for him than yourself, which suggests you do care very deeply for him,' Fernando said quietly.

Ruth didn't want to get drawn into all that again and besides, his tone hadn't indicated anything more than a passing interest.

'It also suggests I'd drunk too much champagne that night,' she laughed lightly. 'Oh, Fernando, do you remember that afternoon we drove out into the country and that drunken peasant fell off his mule, right in front of the car? We got out and this fat peasant woman came screaming out of her white-washed *finca*. . .'

'We thought she'd thought we'd run him down,' Fernando laughed, throwing his head back and holding his forehead.

Ruth was giggling so hard she could hardly get the words out. 'And. . .and she grabbed the rope round the mule's neck and. . .and led it away to safety, leaving her husband lying in the road. What was it she screamed at you, some gypsy curse?'

'Not a curse, more a local proverb about the necessity of keeping a short rope on your mule, your goat and your spouse.'

'And in that order, too,' Ruth laughed, 'because it was ages before she came back for her husband.'

Ruth was still spluttering with laughter when she realised Fernando wasn't. He was just looking down on her face, one hand smoothing the hair from her cheek.

'I should have heeded it as a warning, though, *querida*,' he rasped throatily. 'I should have kept a short rope on you and then you would never have escaped me.'

Slowly he lowered his head down to hers, blocking out the blood-red sky. The kiss was light, delicate, softly sensual and nothing like the prelude to fire and passion and glory. And because of that it tipped Ruth's heart so desperately she curled her arms around his neck and clung to him.

She wanted to cry then, terrible tears of hopelessness, for the kiss and the way he held her so comfortingly *were* hopeless. The suspended despair inside her splintered into a shuddering sob and Fernando tightened his hold on her. He moved his mouth from her lips and pressed it hard against her cheek. They lay together in the gathering darkness, holding each other, neither making any attempt to speak their hurt and their loss but both knowing it was there, buried deep within them.

At last Fernando moved, rolling himself slightly away from her to remove strands of her long hair from his jacket and smoothing them back where they belonged, down the side of her face.

'Beautiful sunset, wasn't it?' he drawled softly.

Ruth smiled. 'I've seen better,' she quipped.

'That's my girl,' he whispered before lowering his lips to hers once again. The poignancy in this kiss on her warm lips nearly induced instant paralysis on every sense of her body. She had expected passion and had been prepared to bluff that away, but this was different. This was a soft seduction of her senses, a sensuous reminder of what they had been to each other and what they had lost. And the irony of it all was that Fernando hadn't planned it that way. She would put her life on it that he hadn't. It seemed he had just given up and was letting her go graciously and tenderly.

Fernando drew away from her and Ruth scrambled to her feet, smoothing the creases from her dress. While he shook out the blanket and brushed down his trousers Ruth turned her pinched face towards the sea. She loved him so very much that if he suggested they take hands and spurt to the cliff-edge and plunge off the edge together like lovesick lemmings she would do it.

She shivered as they started to walk back towards the pine trees, black now and menacing. She wished that Fernando had in fact made fiery, passionate and glorious love to her on that blanket, because at least her body would have been sated and that would have been something at the very least. What she had now was twice what she had suffered before this—a love so very agonising, a love without hope because someone else had the right and the claim to him now and that was

why he had kissed her that way — to let her know how
hopeless it all was.

'I have to go out today,' Fernando told her when she
came down for breakfast on the terrace the next morning. 'I have some meetings in Alcudia.' He shrugged
and smiled at her. 'More hotels,' he added.

Ruth pulled out a wicker chair from the breakfast
table and sat down and helped herself to coffee. 'You
sound apologetic, as if it's a crime to make a few more
million. Go ahead, beaver away, and while you're
negotiating give a thought to my business that will
crumble if I don' get out of here and do some negotiating of my own.'

'Ah, the business, we mustn't forget that.' His tone
was barely sarcastic but hinted at enough to have Ruth
wary again. 'Come with me,' he suggested, leaning
forward to watch her lather a slice of toast with butter
and marmalade. 'Alcudia has an old harbour, a very
fine beach and the old village was built near the site of
a Roman settlement — and there's a museum. We can
do all that and I can introduce you to a few people.'

She was oh, so tempted but. . .'And keep an eye on
me so that I won't escape,' she bit out before biting
into her toast.

'You know the heat is off, Ruth,' he told her, his
eyes catching hers and holding them for a few seconds.

Ruth was the first to break the contact, lowering her
eyes to her coffee-cup. She knew exactly what he
meant, though nothing specific had been said. Their
meal last night had been delicious and the conversation
had flowed and everything had been so very different
from what she had expected. It was their talk on the
cliff-top as the sun had gone down that had changed it
all. Instead of the sunset raging a fire in them as
Fernando had obviously intended, it had had the

reverse effect—doused away a good deal of bitterness and left them with a certain sadness.

'So I'm free to go, am I?' She looked up then and saw a flicker of doubt in his dark eyes and then it was gone and he shrugged.

'I see no reason why you don't use this place as a base. It must surely be better than renting an apartment in a noisy holiday complex.'

'Yes, but. . .' There were no buts when she thought about it. . .apart from one. 'What about Maria Luisa? I don't want to be here when she comes back.'

'She'll give me plenty of warning.'

'That sort of an arrangement, is it?' Ruth said ruefully.

'Yes, that sort of an arrangement,' Fernando replied darkly, slightly annoyed. 'So will you come with me to Alcudia?'

Ruth felt uncomfortable at the request—or was it a challenge, a mini challenge to bring Seville back to her? Choose him in preference to her own work once again?

She stalled. 'Shouldn't you be asking me first if I'm staying?'

He confidently stated with a smile, 'I know you will. So will you come with me?' he repeated.

Ruth lifted her coffee-cup and saucer and leaned back in her chair to sip it. Pity he hadn't shown such confidence before. That was a new thought. Had she lost respect for him for not being so positive and forcing her to stay last year? She could almost laugh at that. Women were certainly complex creatures, wanting their own space, grabbing at it and then grizzling because men weren't crowding them. Women wanted their cake and to eat it too—they were getting more like men every day!

She looked at him over the top of her cup. He was waiting for her answer, not exactly on the edge of his seat, though. He was burrowing in a briefcase while he waited. He looked so refreshed this morning and Ruth resented that. She had slept badly, tossing and turning in the heat though the room had been cool enough. She had burned from inside because she couldn't get out of her mind the thought that Fernando was sleeping under the same roof, so close yet so far. Had his need, like hers, kept him sleepless, the memory of other nights firing his flesh till a cold shower in the middle of the night had been the only relief? The very devil it had!

He looked up suddenly. 'For the third time, will you come with me?'

The question plundered her reverie. Shaking her head, she declined. 'No, but thank you for the offer. I've no need to go to Alcudia, my clients are already sold on Pollensa.' She frowned suddenly. 'If Steve doesn't come back for a few days I'll probably have to go into Palma and see the airlines and the tourist board myself.' She didn't mind but it would put more pressure on her schedule. She put her cup and saucer down on the table. 'Have you any idea when they'll be back?'

'None whatsoever,' he stated flatly.

'You don't even care, do you?' Ruth asked, the frown still playing on her brow. She really didn't understand this side of him. He was taking it all so coolly, his mistress away with a past lover.

'I've told you, I've every faith she'll come back.'

'Because you have that something precious that Steve hasn't got? Don't you be so sure.' She stood up and started to clear the breakfast table.

Fernando stood up too. 'But I am sure, you see, sublimely confident that she will come back to me.'

'And is it that sublime confidence in yourself that prevents you from marrying her? You think she is so besotted with you she'll be content to live with you forever?'

'The subject of marriage has never come up in our

relationship.' He handed her his cup and saucer to pile on a tray.

She bet it hadn't from *him*. 'You surprise me. I wouldn't have thought her class-conscience parents would be very happy with her openly living with a man.'

'Meaning you don't think I'm good enough for her?' He obviously didn't believe that; there was humour glinting in his eyes.

'I didn't mean that, as well you know. I meant that I was under the impression the Spaniards had strong beliefs about virginal brides and the sanctity of marriage and children and a strong family unit.'

'There are always exceptions to the rule,' he said flatly, taking the laden tray from her hands and turning to go along the terrace to the dining-room.

Ruth didn't follow straight away; she stood folding her napkin absently and staring down at it and wondering what she had learnt from that. Very little more than she knew already about their relationship. And the very little was that Fernando showed no signs of missing Maria Luisa or in fact *loving* her very much.

Confused, Ruth went up to her bedroom to change. She'd dressed for breakfast in shorts and T-shirt and it wasn't the ideal outfit for talking business with hotel managers. She really must put Maria Luisa and Steve and Fernando out of her mind and concentrate on what she was here on the island of Majorca for — to work.

Ruth loved the ancient town of Pollensa with its quaint narrow streets and low red stone houses. It was quiet and positively dozy in comparison to Palma. This was the real Majorca, Ruth suspected. In spite of the heat she climbed the supposed three hundred and sixty-five steps to the Calvary, losing count around the end of April so didn't know if it was true or not. She rested now and then under the shade of the cypresses and watched other tourists labouring in the heat. When she finally reached the top she agreed with a young couple from Leeds that it was worth it for the view, which was stupendous in spite of a slight heat haze that hung in the air.

Hunger and a need for sea air drove Ruth down to the Puerto de Pollensa. This was the business end of her trip but before she started she wandered along a crowded beach, taking photographs of the sands, water-skiers and windsurfers, the tree-lined promenade and the backdrop of mountains beyond.

She settled for lunch at a seafront café — an ice-cold Coke and a selection of *tapas*. She sampled *calamares* and *boquerónes* and dipped her bread in the marinade. Fernando's *escaladun* had been wonderful last night and not direct from the freezer. All his own work. She hadn't known he was such a good cook. . . She paid her bill and wandered back to where she had parked the car in a shady spot under an orange tree in a square — She didn't know a lot about Fernando Serra, she realised with a dull bumping of her heart. She knew a lot about his lovemaking technique, though, and that wasn't anything to be proud of.

The huge wrought-iron gates of Casa Pinar were wide open when she got back later that afternoon so she knew Fernando was home. Home, she thought dismally as she drove up the gravelly drive. Not hers but his and the lovely woman he lived with but had no intention of marrying — yet, that was. This enforced separation might make him feel her loss. Absence made the heart grow fonder, some fool once said.

'You didn't tell me about the music festival starting next week in Pollensa — every Sunday for a month in the cloisters of Santo Domingo.' She'd seen some posters in the town and was curious.

Fernando turned to her from the fridge where he was taking out a bottle of wine. He looked as if he'd been home a while. His hair was damp as if he'd been swimming and he was dressed casually in jeans and a thin dcnim-blue shirt. 'It never came up in conversation last night. Would you like to go?' He poured her a glass of wine.

'Yes, if I'm still here,' she murmured under her breath as they went outside to the terrace.

'It was founded by a Yorkshireman, you know.'

'What, the music festival?' Ruth asked incredulously.

'A Philip Newman; he died in 1966. His music festival lives on.'

'That's a lovely thought,' she breathed as they sat in the shade to drink their wine. 'Do you see much of your parents?' she asked, changing the subject; to dwell on concerts with Fernando was too much of a painful reminder of Seville.

'My father died four months ago,' he told her quietly.

Ruth swallowed hard. 'Oh, I'm sorry, Fernando,' she breathed softly. 'You. . .you must miss him. You were close.'

'You remember,' he said softly but not looking at her.

'I remember everything about Seville,' she muttered, more to herself than him. 'How is your mother coping?'

'She's with her sisters on Menorca. Another of the reasons I'm here. I came back when my father was ill and stayed on. This is the family home and my mother didn't want it left empty. She wants to see it a family home once again.'

And it would be, very soon, Ruth thought dismally. When Maria Luisa returned. 'Does. . .does your mother get on with Maria Luisa'?

Fernando smiled and glanced across at her. 'Yes, she is very fond of her. Does that hurt you?'

Ruth shrugged dismissively. 'Why should it?'

'Because once I told you my mother would adore *you*.'

'And now she adores another—that's life!' she

clipped so tightly that it was quite plain she *was* hurt.
She tried to get out of it by standing up and stretching
as if the conversation was threatening to bore her stiff.
'Do you mind if I go for a swim?'

He shrugged. 'You are my guest so you must do as
you please.'

Yesterday she had been his prisoner. How easily she
had let him manipulate the transition.

'I'll go and change into my bikini,' she mumbled.

'Why bother? You didn't yesterday.'

'Yesterday I was under pressure to prove a point.
Today the pressure is off.'

'So all that preening naked on the pool-edge *was* for
my benefit?' he teased.

For the first time Ruth conceded it had been — a
funny sort of rebellious gesture that she'd hoped would
be witnessed.

'And for my own,' she told him with a small smile.
'You know how the sun always turns me on. A plunge
in the pool soon turned me off.'

'Is that why you're going in now — feeling the heat a
bit?' he asked suggestively.

'Not your heat, Fernando. You've lost it,' she told
him bluntly. 'I'm just exhausted after dragging myself
around hotels all afternoon.'

'How did you get on?'

The question surprised her as she had expected him
to pick up on her insult. 'Very well, I have three further
appointments tomorrow afternoon — three hotels who
are interested in offering a good discount, off-season,
of course. I should be able to tie it all up tomorrow.'

He stood up. 'Good, I'm glad to hear you had such a
successful afternoon.'

They both walked into the house together. 'And what
sort of a day did you have? Successful too?' she asked.

He burst out laughing and put his arm around her
shoulder. 'We sound like a married couple.'

In spite of this new plateau of understanding they had reached she still tensed under his touch. He felt it too and let his hand drop to his side.

'Still not quite there, are we?' he grated.

He stopped at the foot of the stairs as if he had just escorted her there and was off somewhere else.

'What do you mean?' Her voice was low as she spoke.

He lifted her chin. 'You do know, so don't pretend you don't. We still care for each other and, try as hard as we might, we still want each other.'

'I don't think that was ever in dispute, Fernando,' she retorted baldly.

'You're right, it wasn't, but something has changed and I'm not at all sure it's for the best.'

She turned her chin out of his reach. 'Well, I can't pretend I know what that means.'

'Last night, the sunset, the meal, the conversation. This morning, this day, this effort at normality. We can go so far, Ruth, and then. . .' His fingers came up and snapped once again and he didn't need to say any more.

Ruth's tongue snaked out to moisten her lips. 'But . . .but we already know that nothing will happen. You said so yourself. All this was a punishment for something I'm still not sure about.'

'It was a punishment for Seville,' he told her flatly.

'It couldn't be anything else! It's all we had!'

'But we could have had much more——'

'If you had come to England as I thought you would have done,' she interrupted frostily.

His dark eyes narrowed. 'That wasn't the reason it all fell apart and you know it.'

Oh God, she did, and how. Ruth lowered her eyes and clutched at the banister of the stairs. 'There are still so many grey areas when I reflect on that trip, Fernando,' she murmured. 'You blame me for return-ing to England because of my job but it wasn't just that and it wasn't all my fault.' Her hand came up to rub her forehead to try and make her think more clearly. She lifted her head to look at him. 'I was afraid. . . I was really afraid that it wasn't the real thing——'

'How could you doubt that?' he insisted, his eyes almost murderous at the suggestion. 'We made love right up until the end,' he reminded her, causing her to draw in her breath raggedly. 'But you knew that you had no intention of ever seeing me again. Your heart had already closed off——'

'I closed off. . .yes, I did close off my heart because you had closed off yours,' she insisted quickly, her words coming in a rush.

'I pleaded with you to stay!' he retorted, suddenly angry with her. 'How could that possibly be misconstrued as closing off?'

'Because you didn't mean it!' Ruth cried, her eyes brimming with tears. She swallowed fiercely. She mustn't cry, she mustn't. 'And you didn't believe for a minute that I would agree and that's why you said it. It made it all right in your eyes. You made the offer, I declined; an easy way out for us both.'

He stared at her; the murderous look had vanished and was replaced by one of sheer puzzlement. 'I don't understand women, I just don't understand them,' he breathed in sufferance.

'And I don't understand you!' Ruth cried. 'You just let me go. You made silly, empty requests and then let me walk out of your life. Now you're trying to make me pay. It's all crazy, absolutely wild!' She turned to rush up the stairs but he caught her wrist. She didn't struggle but faced him angrily. 'What started all this up again, Fernando? We were doing all right, actually getting to know one another as we hadn't known each other in Seville.' She sighed deeply and raggedly and shook her head becauase it was all impossible. 'Don't even tell me——'

'Because you can't face the truth that we are falling in love yet again?' he suggested so calmly that she wanted to slap him hard for his change of mood.

'Don't be so ridiculous! We aren't!' And that was true, for her—she'd never been *out* of love with him and if he was falling for her he couldn't have loved her before. Oh, she had been right to turn down his offer—the affair would never have lasted the year!

'We are,' he insisted, his grip on her wrist tightening, 'and I wish that it weren't happening——'

Ruth interrupted him with an embittered laugh. 'Why, because it interferes with your revenge theme? No, wait a minute.' She held her fingers up and snapped them but her snap wasn't a patch on his. 'I think you've done an about-turn. You've decided you would like to make love to me after all and what better way to do it than trying to win your way into my bed with flattery?'

Now he had the audacity to laugh. 'I don't need to flatter my way there, Ruth. You've already admitted that you would give in willingly.'

'Yes, I did, didn't I? But you daren't take the risk of trying it on in case I was calling your bluff and would refuse *you*. But with all this soft talk of falling in love again you think a refusal wouldn't be a consideration.'

His eyes blackened angrily and Ruth supposed she had been right and exposed him for what he was—a cool bastard.

'I haven't even got that far in the analysis of this new theory but it only adds to my doubts about it all anyway. I repeat, I wish it weren't happening. I wish I could do something to stop it but I'm not going to deny it and you'd be a liar if you tried.'

Her eyes smarted with tears. 'But the difference is, Fernando, that you feel something that I don't——'

'I told you not to try denying it because I won't believe you,' he insisted with iron resolve in the pitch of his voice.

Ruth widened her blue eyes. 'You don't even know what I was about to say!'

'I don't have to. You show your contempt openly.'

She couldn't bear this any longer, this toing and froing of his emotions, tossing her around as if she were in the eye of a tornado. 'And you are blind, Fernando Serra, not totally but enough to be choosy about what you do see. You talk of falling in love *again*. Well, that's the difference between us. I can't fall in love with you again because I've never been out of love with you!' She bit her lip instantly, regretting her outburst as much as she regretted ever catching his gaze at that ill-fated cocktail party. 'Oh, to hell with you!'

She spun to run up the stairs but he caught her and pulled her into his arms. 'Oh, God, Ruth, what the hell are we doing to each other? I didn't mean it to sound like that—that I'd stopped loving you and was falling again.' He pressed her head against his shoulder and smoothed his mouth across her hair.

'It. . .it sounded that way,' she choked against his shirt. Her arms crept around his waist and every last scrap of fight and anger drained fluidly from her body. She couldn't bear any more of this. 'Oh, Fernando, I'm. . . I'm so sick of all this.'

'I know, *querida*,' he whispered throatily. 'I can't bear it having you here and fighting like this and not having you, really having you. I manipulated you here to punish you and you're right—I'm hurting myself as well as you.'

She desperately wanted to talk this out, to grasp these new feelings. He was partly right. They were falling in love, but not again, just in a different way. But in between these new feelings there was a gap of nearly a year and in that time something so terrible had happened. Something so awful she would never be able to put it past her. Fernando had found happiness, with someone else.

'Don't, Fernando,' she breathed achingly as his mouth grazed her cheek on its way to her mouth.

But her lips were already parted, awaiting the warmth and the love he had deprived her of so long.

He moaned submissively as their lips ground hard against each other. His arms tightened around her and desire didn't need to be summoned consciously. It was there within them, a fiery surge of power that raced their breath.

'Please,' Ruth sobbed. 'Not yet, Fernando. There . . .there is. . .is so much to say. . .'

'And we'll say it, *querida*, as we love.'

He swept her up into his arms and Ruth cried out but the cry stayed in her throat, trapped by a sudden rush of need. She clung to him, terrified he would drop her as he carried her upstairs to her bedroom.

To her bedroom, her heart cried out. Not his, because his he shared with her—Maria Luisa. Her name tore through her very soul and not far behind it was Steve's.

The web tangled and clung mawkishly around her reasoning as Fernando lowered her to the bed.

'You. . .you said. . .we. . .would talk,' she breathed feebly. She went to cringe back from him but stilled as he started to unbutton his shirt. The hairs on her arms stood on end as that electrifying pulse of need sparked through her.

'Yes, we'll talk, *querida*,' he rasped through a throat swollen with need. 'I want you. I need you. You haven't been out of my thoughts since the last time we made love. I want to be inside you, pulsing inside you.' He lowered himself down to the bed and her hands frantically flew to his bare chest. 'Is that the sort of talk you want to hear?' he grated hotly against her burning neck.

A sob exploded in Ruth's throat and she pressed the flat of her hands hard against his chest. She struggled to get the words out and when they came they hurt so much.

'Fernando, I can't. . . I can't let this happen. . . You're living with Maria Luisa!'

His whole body tensed and his eyes were so hooded with desire she thought she would never be able to stop him.

'*Querida*,' he said hoarsely, caressing her tumbling hair from her face, 'you know me, you know I wouldn't do anything that wasn't right. Maria Luisa is not in my heart as you think. You are the only one ——'

'But ——'

'No, buts. Trust me, as you trusted me in Seville. Let me love you as I did before. We are together and that is all that matters for now.'

Ruth didn't answer. It was impossible to breathe a word when your heart was so ready for love. She simply spread her fingers across his back and drew him hard against her eager mouth, swollen and throbbing with a need she couldn't disguise.

She did trust him and she knew he spoke from the heart. The tangled web of their past and present balled against the rage of Ruth's emotions. The past didn't matter, the present did, but not the present that included others, just the essential now, the one that was just her and Fernando. They were the *only* consideration.

CHAPTER SEVEN

FERNANDO's whole body was on fire as Ruth tore the shirt from his shoulders. Her lips moved passionately across his chest, tasting and devouring what she had craved for so long.

There was no need for tentative steps of discovery but nevertheless it was as if this were the very first time. The touches and caresses she thought would be so familiar were strange and exciting and erotic.

She moaned softly as he towered above her to loosen her shirt, opening it wide to reveal the lacy silk bra confining her full round breasts. A mist of liquid desire clung to the perfumed skin between her breasts and he lowered his tongue and lips to the tiny oasis of moisture, and as he drew erotically on her flesh his hands moved to the clasp and released her, burying his face against her satin skin as he tore the lace away.

Ruth arched desperately against him as powerfully he slid his hands under her hips and pulled her hard against every muscle that strained feverishly at his jeans. She wanted to tear them from him, to feel his naked flesh against hers, not harsh, unyielding denim. She wanted no restriction between them — not anything material, not any form of mental restriction either. She blocked eveything from her mind, people and places and hurtful thoughts. She thought only of the moment. Her and Fernando, loving, making love as if for the very first time, with urgency and excitement and a fevered rush of emotions.

Fernando tried to slow the pace and Ruth clung to him breathlessly. She wanted it to last too, to make love slowly and languorously, for it to go on forever.

She drew deep breaths and fought for control over her trembling limbs.

Shakily Fernando eased away from her and in that terrible second she hesitated, fearing the rejection he had once threatened her with. His mouth closed swiftly over her anguished lips, to reassure her that his need was real and wouldn't be snatched away from her in a punishing gesture. Relief and remorse for doubting him flooded her as his hands moved to relieve himself of his jeans. She helped him, parting her lips from his to draw breath in her eagerness to remove all that separated them.

There was a ragged pause, not a movement as the last of her underwear floated over the side of the bed. Ruth lay beneath him, inert, gazing up into the dark depths of his eyes. She saw what she was searching for—the deep love she had once known before. It was all she needed to strengthen what he had told her—that Maria Luisa was not in his heart. It still flamed for her and her relief was immense, overpowering the craving for her sexual relief.

So confident now, so sure of him, she let her own heart speak. 'I love you, Fernando,' she breathed so softly that she wondered if he had heard.

His gentle, 'shush!' was confirmation that he had. He ran a tremulous fingertip over her lips in a further gesture to silence her as if he couldn't bear the pain of hearing the words spoken. Ruth understood why in that tender, desperate second. They had used the words so freely in Seville and look what had happened. He didn't want to tempt fate, but fate had brought them together again and now there was only him and her in the whole world.

Fernando looked down on her adoringly before allowing his lips to graze languidly over her mouth and cheeks and throat. She felt faint and tremulous under the sweet pressure and then when his lips grew more demanding the faintness was gone and pure sensual sensation clamoured her senses.

Fernando, his mouth clinging passionately to hers, raised his body away from her to give his hands freedom to move. They moved slowly, effortlessly, stroking her breasts with feather-light touches at first and then deepening the pressure as her flesh burned hotly under his touch. Her breasts swelled, demanding their own fevered release and Fernando knew and understood and lowered his mouth to her inflamed nipples, taking each in turn, drawing and teasing till Ruth squirmed and twisted in ecstasy beneath him.

She gripped his head and held him as his tongue raged circles of temptation till the ache inside was a fearful pain that cried in torment. Ruth careered her hands down his back and pressed her wild body urgently against him till she roused moans of pleasure from deep inside him.

'God, but I want this to last,' he rasped as his mouth came wildly back to hers. 'I want it all, everything I've missed this past year. Your touch. . .touch me, *querida*.'

He gave her space, shifting slightly away from her, his hand coaxing over her midriff. She ran the heated tips of her fingers over his arousal and delighted in the deep shudder of pleasure that racked through him. As she stroked and caressed his own fingertips traced spirals of fire down into her groin. Her legs trembled as his strokes of desire on her thighs crazed her need to fever pitch.

He moved against her hands, jerkily, almost losing the control he had fought to keep down. And then with a desperate movement he drew back from her grasp, his breath rasping in his chest.

'I can't hold back, *querida*. It is impossible.'

With one hand he guided himself into her and Ruth gasped in wonderment, shifting her hips, urging herself to him. His penetration was deep and complete and surged pleasurable pain through her whole body. She twisted her mouth in a cry of sheer ecstasy and bit hard on her lip. Wild primeval instincts took over and her body responded to the deep thrusts of his, trembling and shuddering as his rhythm spun her higher and higher.

Moisture ran from her brow as the fire flourished and crackled and the pressure inside her gathered fearful momentum. She couldn't hold back; like him, it was all impossible. He knew her body, knew her needs, and his timing was perfection. He eased back from her, only allowing himself a partial penetration. He raised himself up from her to look down on her face, to witness the sweet pleasure that parted her lips sensuously and filmed moisture to her brow.

His thrusts quickened, barely inside her, small delicate thrusts that peaked her sensitive pulse again and again. Sharp spasms of erotic pleasure raced her nerve-endings till they screamed for freedom. Her agonised cry of fluid release caused him to cry out with her as her climax broke like a fever, shuddering her whole body as if an electric current had rushed through it, shock-wave after shock-wave of erotic delight.

And as her body and limbs thrummed in the dizzy afterflow Fernando deepened his penetration, shuddering against her till she clung to him, grinding herself under him to give him the ultimate pleasure, to enhance every thrust he pounded into her, to draw him hard down into her power and her love. The final plunge rocked them so unsteadily, their cries were bitten out simultaneously. The swell surged deep inside her, the fire and the passion and the blaze of glory, and as their swollen mouths sought each other they were bonded forever in the secret lair of their love.

When Ruth eventually stirred from her languid torpor it was dark and hot.

'Don't go,' Fernando grated, clutching at her hips to pull her back against his body. Ruth circled her arms around his neck and splayed her fingers through his thick, curly hair. Their bodies were covered in a mist of moisture as they lay side by side. Fernando took the edge of the sheet and patted at the beads of vapour at her brow. 'Did you sleep?' he murmured.

'Did you?' she whispered back, lowering her hands to touch the side of his face.

'I can't remember. Everything went black. Do you think we died?'

She laughed and playfully tugged at his hair and he responded by penetrating her completely with only the slightest of movements.

'Fernando!' she cried in amused astonishment.

'What?' he said mock-innocently and drew away from her as if nothing had happened.

'You're insatiable!' she cried as she pushed him away and slid out of bed.

The bedside lamp snapped on and she turned to see Fernando, raised up on one elbow, gazing at her. 'Don't run away and get dressed,' he pleaded roughly. 'Let me enjoy you. It's been so long, Ruth.'

She didn't want to get sad now, not now after it had been so good. She smiled and stretched her body languorously. 'Take your fill, you voyeur, you,' she teased and almost immediately added, 'That's enough. It will cost you if you want any more.'

'I'll pay,' he laughed back as she reached for her robe.

'You can't afford me,' she giggled as she fled to the bathroom.

The laughter was suddenly gone and a desperate sadness enveloped Ruth as she closed the door after her and leant back against it. She loved him so desperately and she knew he loved her, but maybe not enough. Maybe Maria Luisa was such a deep part of his life now that there was no hope for their future. He had admitted that she wasn't in his heart but she was nevertheless in his life.

She bit her lip and closed her eyes and prayed that she and Steve would somehow resurrect what they had had in Seville as she and Fernando had done. She didn't understand why Maria Luisa was still living with him. She supposed that they had needed each other after Seville and slid into a love-affair but now it had faded. . . But she didn't know and perhaps Maria Luisa was still in love with Fernando. . .but why was she with Steve now? Oh, it was all so confusing.

Horrible thought, but suppose she was just living with him for his money? Fernando had said he was confident she would return because he had something precious that Steve hadn't: was it a serious bank balance?

Ruth sat on the loo and held her head in her hands. Suddenly her whole future happiness hinged on Maria Luisa's choice. Steve or Fernando. It didn't bear thinking about.

'Shall we swim now?' she heard Fernando call out from afar.

Ruth couldn't think straight. She raked her damp hair from her brow as if it would help, but it didn't; she just couldn't think.

'It. . .it's dark,' was all she could offer plaintively.

'Not in my pool, it isn't,' he called back, and she heard the far-off dull thud of a door.

Desolately Ruth went into the bedroom and slid into her bikini and, grabbing a towel from the bathroom, she went downstairs and out through the dining-room door to the terrace.

She didn't want to think any more about choices. She had made her own, to love him again, and it was all she could live with at the moment.

'Oh, Fernando,' she breathed huskily as she stood on the edge of the pool. 'It's beautiful. A mini Hollywood.'

Fernando was already in the water. The pool was lit from below and shimmered the water to a deliciously inviting pale green. And there were soft lights secreted in the rocks, throwing dark shadows and splashes of light into crevices that by day would have been invisible. It was a magical place to be on a hot Majorcan night.

'Oh, no, you don't,' Fernando called out as she dropped the towel and prepared to dive off the edge to join him.

'Don't what?' she laughed, teetering to keep her balance on the edge.

'Off with that bikini!'

'That's not fair!' she protested, stepping back to steady herself.

'It was very fair the other day,' he teased.

She shook her head. 'That was then and why should I swim naked when you —— ?'

Laughter caught in her throat as he up-ended and dived under the water and she caught a flash of very tanned naked rear end.

'OK, you win,' she giggled.

He suddenly emerged from the water, in front of her. 'Hold it,' he grated, sweeping hair and water from his face.

'What now?'

'Slowly, seductively. Tease me, tempt me.'

'Fernando!' she wailed. 'There is nothing seductive and tempting in stepping out of a bikini. Now if I were wearing suspenders and silk ——'

'Get on with it, Ruthie,' he told her, and though he was grinning from ear to ear she knew what was powering him and she felt the excitement blossom in herself.

Ruthie; it was the first time he had called her that

here in Majorca. He had used it a lot in Seville. A sweet, soft, almost childish version of her name. Oh, God, she loved him and needed him.

Grinning, she took up a seductive pose and started to wriggle her hips for him, swirling round sensually and then slowly undoing the clasp at her back. When her breasts were free she teased him with the top half of her peach-coloured bikini, waving it over his head and snatching it out of reach as he stretched up for it. She was laughing and relishing the delicious feeling of her breasts exposed to the warm night air. Already they were aroused and she longed for the water against her overheated skin to caress and tease her further and she longed to plunge in beside Fernando and for him to. . .

She let out a scream as with a triumphant roar Fernando caught the bikini-top and pulled it sharply. She wasn't quick enough to let go and it overbalanced her and she plunged into the water next to him.

She went under completely and on her way down Fernando caught her and raked her all the way down his naked body. His body was hard and fearfully aroused and her skin, cooled by the water, raced with pleasure. She surfaced, gasped for air, and kicked out with a scream of laughter as Fernando grabbed at her bikini-bottom.

Ruth was as agile as a dolphin in the water and she was away from him before he had a chance to stop her. She kicked out of the bikini-bottom that Fernando had succeeded in half tearing from her and struck out for the furthest end of the pool, laughter gripping her and weakening her limbs as he lashed out after her.

She was screaming by the time he caught her, screaming with laughter.

'I didn't know you were such a strong swimmer,' he huffed, trapping her at the side of the pool with his arms each side of her on the bar. They were at the deep end of the pool and both trod water to keep afloat.

'School champion for the breast-stroke,' she panted.

'Me too,' he husked, letting go with one hand and running it across her breasts.

Her mouth parted in laughter again and he filled it with his lips, drawing so passionately on her that her whole body spasmed against him.

Ruth linked her arms around him and wrapped her legs around his.

'Higher,' he grazed as he tore his mouth from hers.

The infusion of desire that rushed her was so immense that she obeyed instantly, drawing her legs up to his hips.

His mouth encompassed hers once again as he drove into her, so shockingly abrupt and yet so incredibly sensual. His tongue thrusting between her impassioned lips emulated the rhythm of his penetration. Ruth's head spun wildly as her whole body convulsed against his.

The water buoyed them and Ruth had never experienced anything so erotic as she dragged her hands down his wet back to grasp his hips to her own. Her mouth sought his again and again as they broke for breath.

'Oh, God, no,' she husked pitifully as Fernando suddenly drew back from her and with eyes hooded with desire and power he let himself sink below the water.

Ruth cried out in despair as his mouth and tongue teased her feminine core. She arched her body and threw her head back against the stone surround. She was going to die with sweet ecstasy and he was going to drown. Suddenly there was a rush of water and he was there and she grabbed at him and then the world and white water spun as he entered her again, deeply, thoroughly, moving so desperately that she moaned against his mouth.

His kiss was whole and complete and her world was whole and complete as their passion erupted and they

clung together as the liquid fire inside them flowed
furiously in its blazing release. Ruth covered his face
and mouth with hot kisses as the fire, for a defiant
instant, raged and then cooled in a delicious aftermath
of cleansing, spring-water tranquillity.

'You. . .' he laboured for breath '. . .you are the
most beautiful lover and the most wonderful swimmer,'
he husked earnestly at her throat as they floated dream-
ily in the water, their bodies limp and sated.

'And you are the school champion diver,' she murmured teasingly.

He laughed against her throat and then teased her by
nipping at her chin.

'And salmon die after doing that,' she added softly,
closing her eyes to the bright moon that shone
overhead.

'What, nibbling chins?'

Ruth pushed him away with a groan and struck out
across the pool, moving lazily and languidly with hardly
any strength left in her body. Fernando pulled himself
out of the pool to sit on the edge to watch her.

She thought she had never been happier, not even in
Seville, which was peculiar because in Seville they had
been free. Now they were tied by this web of tangled
emotions and intrigue. . .no. . .she wouldn't think of
Maria Luisa and. . .no—she *wouldn't*. So why was it
better than before? She didn't know; all she knew was
that she adored him more than before and she wanted
him more desperately, therefore inevitably she was
going to be more hurt than the first time.

Ruth saw that as a deserving punishment for what
she was doing now—having an affair she shouldn't be
having. Fernando wasn't married but he was committed. Ruth turned and lazily swam back to him. But his
commitment wasn't here; she was away with another
man. . . No, she mustn't think of such things again.

His tanned, muscled legs were dangling in the water and Ruth steadied herself by grasping them.

'Are you happy?' He smiled down at her.

Ruth nodded and before she could ask him if he was too he clasped her hands and hauled her from the water into his arms.

'I'm starving,' he stated practically. 'We'll go out for a meal, to a quiet exclusive *mirador* I know with the most spectacular views across to Cabo de Formentor and then we'll talk, really talk.'

He kissed her wet lips, warmly, tenderly, bringing them back to life, and she was lost in her love for him and his for her and she really didn't care if they never talked again.

Ruth exhaled a hugh sigh of relief as she stepped out of the hotel foyer into fierce sunlight and a wall of hot air hit her after the cool of the air-conditioning.

It was all done, the conditions agreeable to both parties. Her clients would be over the moon at the accommodation in this particular hotel. Some incentive to the company's sales staff to increase sales. She felt sure the campaign would be a huge success.

Fernando was waiting for her at the kerbside, leaning against his white convertible Mercedes. He looked fed up and Ruth knew why. She had insisted on making these calls and she had won but there had been no satisfaction in that.

'Successful?'

'Yes, very much so,' she grinned happily as he opened the passenger door for her.

'I could have done it all for you with one phone call if you had let me.' He slid in beside her and started up the engine.

Ruth frowned and scrabbled in her bag for her sunglasses. 'I thought we'd already argued that out last night at the restaurant,' she said tightly. 'I don't need

you to do what I'm quite capable of doing myself. It's
my business, not yours. Damn, I think I've left my
sunglasses behind in the hotel.'

Fernando reached over to the dashboard and with a
wry smile picked up her glasses and handed them to
her.

She could read his mind. It was spelled out in large
print. Women were silly creatures and should be at
home with the washing machine instead of closing
business deals. . . Ruth bit her lip and slammed the
glasses over her eyes. He hadn't been thinking anything
of the sort and last night he had only suggested he could
settle her business for her with a phone call to the
manager, whom he knew well, because he wanted to
take her out today instead of waiting outside hotels for
her.

'Where to?' he asked, pulling out from the kerb.
'Manacor for a string of pearls, Inca for a pair of shoes,
the caves of Drach for a good old-fashioned scare or a
romantic drive out to the peninsula of Formentor?'

Ruth grinned, her humour back. 'I'm too young for
pearls,' she teased, 'and I have shoes enough, but I can
never have enough of romance.'

'Your wish is my command,' he teased.

The drive to the Cabo de Formentor was spectacular.
Some of the hairpin bends had Ruth clinging to her seat
and holding her breath. They stopped at Cala de San
Vicente and admired the pinewoods to the south and
the inviting sandy beach below.

'In Seville you said Majorca was greener and lusher
and cooler but you didn't tell me how spectacular and
beautiful it was,' Ruth breathed.

'Or crowded,' Fernando bemoaned as nevertheless
he gathered her into his arms.

'Fernando!' she protested, but still gave in to the
rapture of his embrace and his warm lips on hers. A
youth in Union Jack shorts and nothing else whistled

approvingly and they laughed and sauntered back to the car.

'I wish I'd brought my bikini,' Ruth moaned as she clipped on her seatbelt. 'The sea down there looks so inviting.'

'I'm glad you didn't. I couldn't bear the world whistling at your lovely body.'

'Jealous?' she teased.

'Obsessively so.'

Fernando drove on and Ruth lapsed into a silence of awe. It was all so lovely. The road suddenly descended into a valley shaded by pines and oaks. Fernando pointed out the sheltered Formentor beach and the flowered terraces of the grand Hotel Formentor. They drove on through a tunnel and then the landscape became more arid. Mountain crests rose impressively high and the valleys were deep. They parked and walked to the cape where there was a terrifying sheer drop to the sea.

There were numerous tourists admiring the incredible views but to Ruth there was no one in the world but Fernando. The warm wind blew her hair from her face and she gazed out across the sea where craggy pitons struggled up from the blue sea.

'I can understand your love for this part of the island,' she mused.

'It appeals to the savage side of my nature,' he told her.

'I didn't know you had one.'

'I'll show you tonight,' he whispered roughly in her ear and followed that threat up by nibbling at her earlobe till she giggled helplessly.

'No tour would be complete without a look at the caves,' he suggested, after Ruth had exhausted every adjective she knew at the beauty of the Cape. 'Can you bear it?'

'With you as my guide I could suffer the fires of hell.'

He looked rueful as they walked back to the car. 'You might not be far from the truth in that conjecture,' he told her mysteriously.

Some time later she understood why. Ruth clung to him as her wide eyes drank in the nightmare splendour of the illuminated stalagmites and stalactites. The coolness of the caves shocked her, as did the immenseness of the place.

'It's so huge!' she gasped. 'Drach is the Catalan for dragon, isn't it? Do you think any actually lived here?'

'I think the devil himself and his sisters lived here,' Fernando suggested and Ruth tightened her grip on his arm and gave a small shudder.

Fernando pointed upwards. 'Can you see the cathedral?'

'Where?' Ruth gasped, following his direction. She frowned up at the strange twisted forms of rock that were brilliantly lit by concealed coloured lights. 'It doesn't look like a cathedral to me.'

'Perhaps not,' Fernando laughed. 'Perhaps the cathedral is round the corner and that is the Taj Mahal.'

'Look,' Ruth grinned, 'if you're going to fool around I'm going to join that tour guide over there——'

He gathered her into his arms and kissed and her and then whispered, 'It wouldn't be the same though, would it?'

'Maybe not but at least I'd learn something about these caves.'

'I'll teach you everything you ever need to know.'

'But not about the caves,' she laughed and, tugging at his arm, she insisted they tag on with the other tourists.

'You see,' she whispered later, 'you didn't know that some of those pools are salty because of the sea filtering through the limestone——'

He grinned at the enthusiasm 'Or that Martel, a French speleologist, was the first to explore these caves in 1896. The lake is named after him and if we don't hurry we'll miss the concert.' He grabbed her hand and hurried her after the group who were moving down to take their seats beside the long deep Lago Martel.

Ruth heard music in the distance and then a boat came into view, moving eerily across the limpid waters. The musicians on board played violins and Ruth had never heard anything like it before. Because of the translucent water and the high, rocky, almost petrified appearance of the cave's formation it added a mysterious uniqueness to the beautiful strains of the music.

She gripped Fernando's hand as suddenly her eyes filled with tears of emotion. There was something so moving about the whole experience. There was a deathly hush, no sound but the beautiful music rising up and swirling above them to the glittering pointed icicles in the illuminated cavernous roof.

After a while the floating orchestra glided away but no one moved. Several boats had followed and were waiting to transport the tourists back to a civilisation that seemed so very far away from the respite of these fascinating caves.

Ruth trailed her fingers in the icy water and stared down at the weird rock formations below the surface of the crystal-clear water. Her tears were gone now and she raised her head to look at Fernando. He smiled at her and because they weren't alone they didn't speak but words weren't needed to exchange emotions shared.

'It really is the most beautiful place on earth,' Ruth was still enthusing as she bearded mussels and washed prawns for the paella Fernando had promised her. 'So green and lush and so spectacular and —'

'All right, all right. You've told me a million times how beautiful my island is,' Fernando laughed, sautéing garlic and onions.

'Yes, but you take it all for granted because you live

here. You didn't even wax lyrical about the incredibly romantic island we could see from the cliff-top at the cape. And the caves. They were amazing, unreal and incredibly romantic too.'

'No, my romantic eyes were somewhere else.' He pushed aside the pan and went to her by the sink, wrapping his arms around her waist and pulling her back against him.

'Hmm, you smoothie,' Ruth sighed on a smile and leaned back into him. She was enjoying this, cooking a meal together. It was something they had never done before.

He squeezed her affectionately. 'It's good to have you here, *querida*. I never thought it would happen.'

Ruth shook her wet hands into the sink and swivelled into his arms, gazing up into his face with so many questions milling in her head. She knew he cared, he showed it, but he wouldn't say the things she wanted to hear—that he cared for her to the exclusion of all others, and wanted her in his life to the exclusion of all others. She wanted him to plead with her to stay with him, forever, as he'd done once before, but this time she would accept and tell him how wrong she had been the first time.

'Fate brought us together again, Fernando. Steve believes in fate. . .' She felt the very slightest of tension in his muscles and wished she hadn't mentioned him. They had quite successfully avoided talking about those two lately but some time they would have to—that was if Fernando's intentions were serious. Oh, God, they must be, Ruth's heart told her. Was he simply scared of committing himself once again, in fear of a second rejection? Her heart hammered. She hadn't rejected him the first time, though, just evaded a decision, wanting him to strengthen it somehow. But he was doing nothing to strengthen it now, and was that because of Maria Luisa?

She linked her arms around his neck. 'Why did you tense like that when I mentioned Steve?' she asked softly. There was no point in evading the issue any longer. It had to be talked about.

He frowned and his eyes darkened dangerously and Ruth thought she had misjudged her timing and he wasn't ready for any thoughts of their future together.

'Because it has been good not having anyone else in our lives.' His eyes softened. 'I don't want to think about Maria Luisa or Steve or anyone but us. I don't even want to think about the future.' ·

It wasn't what Ruth wanted to hear. It was nice to know he felt good about her being here but she wanted more than that—but how selfish of her to expect any more. She drew on her lower lip. She'd turned down the only chance she had had.

'Nor I,' she murmured. 'But it's necessary, Fernando.' She widened her blue eyes appealingly. 'I'm being very brave now,' she told him, holding his eyes. 'I want to talk about us and Steve and Maria Luisa. They're a part of our lives and so is the future and some time soon——'

'And some time soon you will have to return to England.'

A cold shiver ran down Ruth's back and she moved out of his arms, quite easily, she noted miserably. Already he was beginning to cool off. That regrettable reminder that people existed outside the Casa Pinar had cooled everything to fast-freeze point. 'Yes, I will, won't I?' she said stiffly, slamming the paella pan back on the stove.

'It's inevitable,' she heard behind her.

Ruth swung to see his eyes had changed to cold hostility and the set of his jaw was so damned determined it chilled her to the very marrow of her bones. Suddenly everything was so deadly serious.

'And what exactly do you mean by that?' Ruth asked

him with trepidation, half anticipating a sudden dis-
missal of herself from his home.

He didn't answer, just stood there with his bronzed
arms crossed across his chest and watched her as if by
staring at her so intently it was answer enough. 'Well,
aren't you going to give me a clue as to what's going on
in your mind?' she went on. 'I'm not a mind-reader,
you know.'

'Neither am I, *querida*,' he said slowly, 'but I wish
that I'd had those skills in Seville because it would have
saved a lot of anguish. Seville was unreal, Ruth.' He
unfolded his arms and turned to tip spices and chicken
and cubes of pork into the pan. He stirred them jerkily,
tossing the meat over to seal it. 'Not a real world at all.
A world created by man to stimulate fantasy.'

'Most didn't see it that way,' uttered Ruth, her heart
beating so hard that *it* was unreal. 'Most people would
say an Expo was to promote, to show the world what
everyone has to offer.'

'Not exactly the way we saw it, though,' he com-
mented ruefully. Ruth handed him a packet of rice and
a jug of stock.

'What did we see, Fernando?' she tempted.

He turned to face her. 'I think we saw pure fantasy.'

Ruth's narrowed her blue eyes. 'In each other?' she
forced a smile. 'You Peter Pan, me Tinkerbell?'

He threw handfuls of rice into the pan followed by
the stock and the sizzle and smell of garlic and spices
filled the kitchen. He put the lid on the pan and picked
up his wine glass and drank before saying anything else.

It gave Ruth time to think and worry. Was he trying
to say that they couldn't recapture what they once had
because it hadn't existed?

'Something like that,' he murmured at last.

Ruth shook her head, not wanting to believe that. 'It
was real enough, Fernando. Don't ever believe that it
wasn't.'

'What was I to believe then when you didn't stay?
When you walked out on me for your career and your
partner?'

'I. . . I didn't ——'

'You did,' Fernando insisted, not harshly but firmly
enough to have Ruth wondering if she actually had.

'I wish we had a tape recording of our last night
together ——'

'Dear God, did it mean so very little to you that you
can't remember every last detail of it?' he questioned
derisively.

His tone suddenly irritated her. 'It was because it
meant so much that I *can't* remember!' she protested.
'All you could think of was yourself, just expecting me
to drop my former life for yours. Life isn't that easy. I
don't remember saying no, what I do remember is the
confusion in my mind. I loved you for thirteen days of
my life, and didn't the rest of my life count for
anything?'

His dark eyes narrowed. 'There was no doubt in *my*
mind, no confusion, simply a compulsion to live the
rest of my life with you.'

His words hurt her and she reached for her wine and
dropped her gaze to the ruby-red liquid. 'You were in
your own country, among your own kind when you felt
that compulsion and made your demands on me. I was
far from home ——'

'And wondering if what you were feeling was infatuation, a holiday romance?' His words were
contemptuous.

Ruth shook her head and then with her free hand
scooped her hair back from her face. She looked at
him, her blue eyes wide and stinging with curbed tears.
'I never thought that, Fernando, not once when I was
with you ——'

'But you did when you got back to England?'

Ruth shook her head. 'No, not even then ——'

'So why, Ruth, why the hell didn't you sort out your affairs and come back to me?'

Ruth let out a twisted laugh and shook her head in disbelief. 'And what would I have found if I had? You and Maria Luisa already living together, both feeling sorry for yourselves and finding a sympathetic shoulder to cry on.' She slammed down her wine glass on the table and held her palms out to him. 'I'm sorry, I shouldn't have said that because it isn't the issue here. What is the issue is that you expected me to stay and I didn't. I've told you before. I expected you to come after me, I prayed you would so that I would know for sure that you really wanted me, but you didn't. You blame me, I blame you. It was six of one and half a dozen of another.' She raked her hair feverishly from her forehead again. 'I don't know what the answer is, Fernando. I really don't.'

Fernando said nothing, offered her nothing, not even a look of understanding. Biting back a sob, she left him shaking the paella pan and went outside to the terrace where the air was fresher. Candles burned on the table where they were to dine and as she sat down at the table she banished the sob for evermore. She sighed and then inhaled the sweet scented air. Would they ever resolve this, and if they did, what then?

She felt his hands on her shoulders and her hands instinctively covered his. Fernando leaned down and planted a soft kiss on the top of her head.

'Fernando,' she whispered, swivelling to face him. He squatted down beside her and took one of her hands in his and waited for her to go on. 'Steve and I talked about all this in the restaurant the other night. . .' His grip tightened. 'No, listen, Fernando, it's very relevant to what we're talking about. We said that we understood things could happen in a glamorous environment——'

'Things?'

'Falling in love, then. We did it, fell in love in a love-inducing environment.'

'I told you it was unreal.'

'But for me and Steve it wasn't. And perhaps it wasn't for you and Maria Luisa. . .' She let her voice trail away to give him space to respond and he did.

'I loved you too, Ruth,' he offered sensitively, stroking her hand as he said it. 'And Maria Luisa loved Steve, and yet it all went wrong for all of us.'

'I know,' she nodded, 'and that was what we were trying to work out.'

'And did you come to any conclusion?'

'We did.' She gave out a long sigh. 'We're different, Fernando.' She just saw the slight frown on his brow by candlelight. 'It's a question of pride, I think. You were too proud to run after me. . .' He smiled and shook his head. 'No, don't laugh, it's true,' Ruth insisted. 'You expected me to drop my life and my career for you because that's what a Majorcan girl would have done.'

Fernando laughed out loud and when he'd finished he clasped her hand to his lips. 'Maybe my father would have expected that but certainly not this generation of Serras. But yes, you are partly right. I did expect you to drop everything for me and when you didn't I didn't run after you, not because I was too proud to but because I was afraid, just as you were afraid. It's not a female prerogative to feel insecure and afraid.'

'I can't imagine you feeling that way,' she murmured.

'You did once say I was old-fashioned and I suppose in some ways I must be. For a time I saw the folly of the recklessness of our affair. It could have had disastrous consequences. . .an unwanted. . .' He shrugged dismissively. 'Let's forget this. For the time being I don't want to go on arguing——'

'Discussing,' Ruth interrupted. 'We aren't arguing. Fernando, we are being very sensible and talking about this as we should have done last year.'

He nodded. 'Yes and now it's. . .' He stopped and Ruth's heart froze because she was sure he was going to say it was too late. Sensing her discomfort, he quickly went on, 'Time to eat.' He stood up and drew her out of her seat with him and gathered her into his arms. His kiss was tender and Ruth slid her arms around his neck and returned the warmth. It wasn't too late, she was convinced of that. Fernando loved her and she loved him and they were meant to be together. All she had to do was get him to repeat what he had said in Seville — that he wanted her to stay, and she would. This time she would.

There was only a very slight frown on her brow when Fernando went inside to bring out the paella. Maria Luisa. Where oh, where did she stand in his life? She didn't know but what she did know was that Fernando wouldn't do anything to hurt anyone. . .only herself, as he had threatened when she had first arrived here at the lovely Casa Pinar. But it was all different now. Wasn't it?

CHAPTER EIGHT

'You can't possibly drive into Palma with a leg like that,' Fernando insisted.

Ruth squirmed as Fernando changed the dressing. 'An ankle like that, not a leg,' Ruth corrected. 'Don't you know your anatomy?'

'Very well, especially yours,' he teased, running his hand up the length of her very sun-gilded leg to her thigh.

'Don't you dare!' she squealed, trying to push him off the edge of the sun-lounger and into the swimming-pool, which was how the accident yesterday had happened, fooling around by the poolside like a couple of kids when Ruth had slipped on a supposedly non-slip surface and wrenched her ankle. 'I'm an invalid now and don't you forget it!' she added, attention-seeking.

'Invalid and invalid as in having no effect,' Fernando grumbled as he went to pour her a drink from a jug on the table.

'Void and null,' Ruth muttered under her breath and she tried in vain to move her ankle without pain. As void and null as her feeble attempts to find out what he didn't want to tell her the night of the paella. It was something to do with Maria Luisa that was all she knew, but Fernando was as tight as a clam. She'd find out soon enough, he'd said gravely once or twice, and that was it.

'You could drive me into Palma,' Ruth suggested in a small voice.

The last couple of days had been wonderful. Fernando had driven her all over the island. They'd climbed down to rocky secluded coves and bathed in

crystal-clear waters and picnicked in shady pine forests.
They had seen the windmills of which there were dozens
on the plains in the interior of the island. Some of the
inland villages stood still in time and were quiet and
peaceful respites from the glamour of the coastal
resorts.

Ruth was in love with the island, all of it, and
Fernando had been the perfect, loving guide and everything was looking so good. . .but now this wretched
ankle business had made her feel utterly miserable and
vulnerable. She'd spent an uncomfortable and restless
night, Fernando insisting on sleeping apart from her.

That had been bad enough but the sleepless night
had got her worrying about her work. There had been
no word from Steve or Maria Lisa and though there
was no time element concerned with this contract she
was still a little worried that nothing had been accom-
plished with the airlines and tourist board in Palma.

Fernando brought her a drink of orange juice and
one for himself and pulled up another lounger next to
her. He sprawled out in his shorts and drank thirstily
before fervently putting down her suggestion.

'No, I couldn't possibly drive you back to Palma.
You need rest and besides, I want you here with me
anyway. I love having you around.'

'You just don't want me to carry on my business, do
you?' she hit back, angered at his refusal and refusing
to see the rest as a compliment.

'Don't start that again, Ruth, or I'll manually wrench
your other ankle *after* I've spanked your backside for
suggesting that I am keeping you from your work. For
the last time, I'm not prejudiced about women working.
If you were married to me I wouldn't expect you to be
bound to the house all day, every day. I'd like you to
do something of your own——'

If she were married to him. How could he make
remarks like that so lightly? 'Does Maria Luisa still fly?'

Ruth interrupted petulantly, refusing to give the mention of marriage a thought.

Fernando narrowed his eyes at her. 'Why do you ask?'

'"Why do you ask?"' Ruth mimicked in disbelief. 'I would think that's obvious—I want to know. She and Steve have disappeared off the face of the earth. If she has a job I would think it was in jeopardy by now.'

'She could be on leave,' he suggested evasively.

Ruth wasn't fooled. 'She damn well isn't,' she struck back heatedly. 'You made her give up her work when she came to live with you, am I right?' Suddenly Ruth felt very vindictive. Her ankle was aching badly and she was hot and very fed up. She'd slap Steve when he got back for leaving her like this. Supposing Fernando hadn't been around? She'd have been stuck in some noisy complex in Pollensa and then had to drive back to Palma to do his share of the work. 'Am I right?' she repeated, dying for a row to ease the tension.

'Absolutely,' Fernando replied tightly as he got to his feet. 'And she did it willingly. . .'

'You see, you are a chauvinist. You put the screws on her and she submitted.'

'So would you have done in the circumstances,' he said wearily, not wanting to get drawn into an argument. 'Now I'll leave you to rest and incubate some more venom while I go and make some phone calls——'

'Well, phone subservient Maria Luisa while you're at it and find out when she is coming back because I'm fed up with. . .with. . .'

'With what?' Fernando challenged drily, daring her to suggest anything—suggestive.

'With loading the dishwasher!' she retorted.

He snorted and walked away.

'Fernando,' she called out as he reached the terrace. She turned and saw he had stopped. He swivelled to

face her with a look of forced tolerance on his face.
'I'm sorry,' she told him, truly regretting her outburst.
'I didn't mean to bite at you so. I'm just fed up with
this ankle and. . .and I shouldn't be here.'

He came back to her and crouched down beside the
lounger and took her hand in his to stroke it. 'I know
you are worried about your work but you can't go
limping around Palma like that. It's too hot and it
wouldn't be good for you and you would hardly look
very impressive with a great bandage twined round your
ankle like the beginnings of a mummifying session.'

She failed to pick up on his humour which he was
putting on to cheer her up. 'Is that the only reason you
won't drive me there?' she asked in a little-girl-lost
voice again.

He smiled. 'The only reason, and I think it's fair
enough, don't you?'

She nodded meekly. 'It wasn't what I meant anyway,
about not being here.'

'So, what did you mean?'

'I. . . I meant that this is Maria Luisa's home
too——'

'This is *my* home, Ruth.'

'But she lives here, with you,' Ruth emphasised, 'and
I shouldn't be here.'

He graced her with a rueful smile. 'A bit late for all
that now, isn't it? If you had a conscience at all you
should have thought about it sooner.'

'I did and you told me to trust you and I did, and I
do, but you won't tell me anything——'

'Because it has nothing to do with you,' Fernando
insisted.

Ruth turned away and groped for her sunglasses and
clamped them over her face so he wouldn't see the hurt
in her eyes. 'So it has nothing to do with me,' she
blurted. 'OK, now I know where I stand—absolutely
nowhere!'

He kissed her lightly on the cheek and she flinched away from him. He stood up and tousled her hair playfully and she refused to look up at him.

'Darling Ruth, if you don't know how I feel about you now, you never will, but now isn't the time for us to make rash statements as we did in Seville. Everything is very different now, there are new considerations, and until I know exactly what is going on you're not going to draw me on the subject.'

Furiously Ruth tore her glasses from her face and glared at him. 'I know why you're doing this,' she reproached scornfully. 'It's because I wanted you to drive me into Palma so I can get on with my work. . . don't walk away from me, Fernando!'

He did; without a word he walked away and didn't look back.

Damn! Damn! Damn! Ruth cursed. Him and his insufferable chauvinism. He claimed he hadn't any but he jolly well had! She eased herself out of the lounger and plopped down by the edge of the swimming-pool and plunged her aching foot, bandage and all, into the cool water. The relief was immense and she wondered if she plunged her brain into the water it would help too. Perhaps she was being silly in thinking that her job was the stumbling-block between them; it was a pebble in the path certainly, but Maria Luisa was the actual stumbling-block. Was he just waiting for her to return so he could choose one or the other of them? Oh, heavens, she was going delirious with this ankle. Fernando loved her, not Maria Luisa, and she *must* be more of a patient patient.

She heard Fernando returning across the patio, jangling car keys in his fingers. 'I have to go out; can you live without me for a couple of hours?'

'I lived a year without you,' she snapped back, swishing her feet in the water.

He walked away without responding to that and Ruth

just hated it when he left her snappy bitchiness hanging in the air with no place to go.

The pool water was working wonders on her ankle and after a few more minutes she tested its strength. It still throbbed a little but was much better. Tomorrow it would be possible to drive and drive she would, back to Palma and the apartment.

She sighed raggedly. Fernando wouldn't like that and she wanted to please him, not anger him, though it took some doing getting his anger up. He was what her mother would have described as a good man. Apart from loving him to distraction it was one of the reasons she was still here. She shouldn't be here because of Maria Luisa but she trusted Fernando enough not to be too unduly worried about it. He wouldn't have wanted her to stay if he was seriously bonded to Maria Luisa. But there was a tie between them all the same. She so desperately wanted to know what was going to happen when she returned.

Hobbling indoors, Ruth went to Fernando's study. She'd call the apartment in Palma in case by a miracle Steve had returned. She picked up the unfamiliar phone clumsily and by mistake depressed the re-dial key. She was about to put the receiver down when the clicks stopped and Steve's voice answered. In terror Ruth dropped the receiver down on to its cradle. That was impossible! Her heart started to hammer against her ribs, her brain went into overdrive. The last call made on that phone was to Steve. . .by Fernando! Without thinking she snatched up the phone again and quickly tapped out the apartment number. It rang forever. Steve couldn't have gone straight out so quickly, it had only been seconds before she had called again. Slamming down the receiver once again, she instantly let out a groan of dismay.

'Idiot!' she shouted to herself. Now if she re-dialled she would only get the apartment ringing incessantly;

the call before she had lost and she hadn't a clue where its destination was. Fool, she should have spoken to Steve, asked him where he was and what the devil he thought he and Maria Luisa were playing at.

Three hours later, hot and frustrated with waiting, she tackled Fernando as soon as he pulled up in front of the house.

'Before you went out you called Steve. Why didn't you tell me you had spoken to him? When are they coming back? What's happening?' she cried.

'Has he called here?' Fernando asked, a frown puckering his brow as he rounded the Mercedes to the boot and opened it wide.

'No,' Ruth told him as she limped towards him. Quickly she explained about the phone call.

His eyes darkened as he thrust the cool-box towards her. Ruth grabbed it and blurted, 'I know what you're thinking. You think I did it on purpose, that I was checking up on you.'

'Your ankle appears to have made a remarkable recovery,' he said caustically, switching the subject.

'Forget my ankle. You do believe I did it on purpose. Well, I didn't, Fernando, you must believe me. I was just clumsy and it happened.'

He swung carrier bags of groceries to the ground before slamming shut the boot of his car. 'I wonder how many suspicious wives have caught out errant husbands with that trick?' He picked up the bags and went into the house.

'I'm not your wife and if I were I wouldn't be suspicious anyway. Well. . . I would if you gave me reason to be. . .like. . .like witholding information from me!' Ruth blazed, limping after him and struggling with the cool-box.

'Leave that where it is,' he ordered, 'I'll come back for it. For heaven's sake get your weight off that ankle and rest it.'

Ruth dropped the box and left it in the middle of the dining-room and stormed after him, her weak ankle totally forgotten in her fury. 'I *didn't* do it on purpose and so what if I had? You've been talking to Steve and I want to know——'

'Such a deducing mind,' he grated, giving her his full attention now. 'But has it occurred to you that you are totally off-target?'

'Off-target!' Ruth spluttered. 'I know whose voice I heard on the other end of the line.'

'Yes, Steve's; full marks for being so quick on the uptake. Nought for presuming I was talking to him when I made that call.'

Ruth went pale. 'Maria Luisa?' she croaked stupidly. And stupid she was. Of course, he'd been talking to Maria Luisa; he had nothing to say to Steve.

'Yes, Maria Luisa,' Fernando said lethally. 'And as she and Steve are together it's not unlikely for him to pick up the phone if it rang.'

'Yes. . .yes, I suppose you're right,' she breathed, feeling very sorry for herself. She'd made it worse. Now she knew that Fernando was in contact with Maria Luisa and probably had been right from the off. It was probably why he wasn't at all worried that she hadn't returned yet. He knew she was safe and well. . . nevertheless.

'I still think you should have told me!' she suddenly flared. 'After all, Steve is my partner and. . . Ohh!' Her ankle gave under her and she clutched at the fridge for support. Fernando caught her before she slid to the floor. He swept her up into his arms with a moan of concern, or was it despair that she was acting so childishly? Cross with herself and deflecting it to him, she hammered at his shoulders.

'Put me down!'

'Certainly not!'

'Where are you taking me? What do you think you're doing?' she screeched.

'Putting you to bed before I lose my temper and toss you into the pool I left you beside. I've had quite enough of your tantrums since you slipped yesterday and I'm getting bored by them. You're a woman, not a child, though that is hard to believe at times.'

She clung to him as he charged up the stairs and into her bedroom where he unceremoniously dumped her on the bed. She was so shocked she was struck speechless.

'Cool off, Ruth,' he ordered sharply and was about to slam out of the room when her speech came back in a rush and furiously she hit out with her *pièce de résistance*.

'Why is the west wing of this house closed up?'

Slowly Fernando turned and in that fearful second Ruth thought she had gone too far. His hand tightened on the side of the door till she could see the whites of his knuckles this far away.

'Checking my phone calls, checking my house —'

'I wasn't,' Ruth denied firmly. 'The phone was a mistake. I didn't mean to do it and you must know that I wouldn't stoop so low —'

His eyes were expressionless, not angry, not cool, not anything in particular. 'All right, so you made a mistake, but it got you going, didn't it? Aroused your curiosity till you just had to find out more —'

'No, it didn't! I was bored while you were out. I'm not used to sitting around doing nothing. If I was curious it was only to see the rest of the house. I like the furnishings and I was interested in the architecture. I. . . I found rooms locked. What have you got to hide, Fernando?' Ruth challenged him hotly.

He offered no denials, which made Ruth feel ten times worse for her accusations. She was being so ghastly and there was probably a very good reason for those locked rooms, if only he would tell her what they were.

She managed to struggle to her feet and cross the room to him barely limping at all. She didn't touch him but stood so close that she would be able to read every facial expression if he chose to lie to her. But he wasn't a liar, she knew, yet he was evading so much and she wanted to know.

'Please tell me what's going on, Fernando,' she implored, her eyes so wide and bright that he couldn't refuse her—surely? 'It just isn't fair that you don't tell me things. You are in touch with Maria Luisa and she's with Steve and he's my partner, not yours. You must know what he and Maria Luisa are planning to do and when and if they're coming back. We've had such a wonderful time these past days——'

'Yes, it has been wonderful, *querida*,' he agreed quietly, his eyes softening till they were almost hazel in shade. 'And I want it to go on the same way till I'm free to offer you more.'

He reached for her and she slumped into his arms. She felt the beat of his heart against her breast but it only came halfway to comforting her. It beat so fast as if he was under a strain. He felt tense too, his muscles bunched hard under his thin shirt as she ran her hands across his shoulders. She turned her face up to his.

'It's because I love you, Fernando, that I'm so paranoid. There's so much about your relationship with Maria Luisa that you won't talk about——'

'Because I can't, Ruth,' he insisted gently. 'It's not mine to share with you.'

'You. . .you mean she comes first, before my feelings?'

She desperately waited for his answer and it looked as if he was fighting an inner turmoil as to what to tell her. His face was so tense as he held her and gazed deep into her eyes.

'For the moment she needs me more than you do,' he said at last.

Her heart beat erratically at that but she managed to shake her head in disbelief. 'She's with Steve, Fernando, not with you——'

'But she has been with me since Seville and you just can't sweep the last year away and forget it,' he told her earnestly. He smoothed her hair with the back of his hand. 'You know how I feel about you——'

'That's just it,' she interrupted in a small, hesitant whisper. 'I don't know how you feel, not exactly. I. . . I keep expecting you to. . .' She couldn't finish because that would be pushy if she admitted she expected him to ask her to stay with him as he had done once before. She feverishly thought that this time, though he was tender and romantic at times, he was being very cautious about his feelings for her. They had hurt each other once and this second time around they were so tentative. She thought she understood, but understanding could be so difficult at times.

She slid her arms up around his neck and his mouth came down to hers. He didn't even question what she had been about to say.

His lips were impassioned and she swum dizzily in the swarm of love that buzzed through her. Once again she wanted to block off the part of her mind that needed to question his past life with Maria Luisa. But perhaps they still had a future life together. Perhaps she would come back and want to pick up with Fernando where she had left off. Oh, no, not that, she wouldn't be able to suffer that, not after the past few days that had been so ecstatic.

'We'd better get that cool-box unpacked before it melts,' Ruth breathed as Fernando moved his lips from her mouth to her throat.

'It can wait, I can't,' he murmured throatily, taking her lips once again. His hands moved determinedly against her blouse, caressing her naked breasts through the thin cotton. Then his hands came around her and gently he lifted her and carried her back to the bed. This time he didn't throw her down with a fury but gently laid her down among the downy pillows and started to strip off his shirt.

'My ankle,' she whimpered pathetically, her eyes dancing with mischief.

'I'm not going to make love to your ankle,' he breathed heavily as he came to lie down beside her, passionately gathering her into his arms.

'Hmm,' Ruth sighed. 'You certainly have mastered your anatomy,' she told him admiringly as he slid his hands across the small of her back to find that ecstatic erogenous zone that never failed to set her on fire.

'Do you have to go today?' Ruth asked as Fernando reached down and grasped her tightly round the wrist to haul her out of the swimming-pool. She'd taken to having an early morning swim to strengthen her ankle, which was doing fine. Most times Fernando joined her, this morning he hadn't. She knew he had an early appointment with one of his lawyers and hoped that that was what was distancing him from her this morning. But she had her doubts. She suspected it was all her own fault. She'd been fractious lately and just couldn't shake off thoughts and doubts about him and Maria Luisa. She was transferring her anxieties to him and now that she recognised that she wanted to do something about it. If he stayed home today she would be sweet and loving. . .and trusting.

Fernando smiled thinly as he cocooned her in a fluffy towel and rubbed her back to dry her. 'It's usually me imploring you not to go to work.'

'You've never implored in your life,' Ruth murmured, resting her wet head on his shirt for a second before pulling away and perching on the edge of the

lounger. 'I'll give it up, you know, everything,' she told
him as she absently towelled her wet hair. 'My partnership, any interest in the company, if. . .'

'If what?' he urged when Ruth let the sentence trail
off like the vapour trail of the jet high in the deep blue
sky overhead. She'd gone too far. He wasn't ready for
this yet.

Ruth flopped back in the lounger and studied the
vapour trail through half-closed eyes. If he married her,
she wanted to say. She wasn't going back to England,
not this time. She was going to stay with him because it
was where she belonged — if he asked.

She lost her nerve at the last minute. 'If you'll take
me to the concert in the cloisters at Pollensa this
weekend.'

'I'll see if I can get tickets,' was all he offered before
kissing her sweetly on the mouth and going inside to
get some paperwork together for the meeting with his
lawyer who was driving out from Palma to see him.

'I'll cook you something wonderful tonight,' she
called after him but he didn't hear.

Later she made herself a light salad for lunch and ate
it on the terrace. She was miserable, she decided. This
lotus-eating life was doing nothing for her. She felt
insecure, unsure of the future and desperately worried
about Steve and Maria Luisa. They'd been gone for so
long now. But every time she mentioned them to
Fernando he assured her they were quite capable of
looking after themselves and promptly closed the subject. He knew something, probably everything, but he
wasn't letting on.

She'd phoned the apartment umpteen times, always
in secrecy, but never got an answer. Now that her ankle
was better she should really go back and chase up on
the calls Steve should have made in Palma so that it
was all tied up when he got back but she didn't want to
spoil it all with Fernando.

It was so good, being with him. In one way their love had got stronger yet absurdly it wasn't quite right and the outcome of their renewed affair she couldn't foresee. Steve and Maria Luisa were the Damocles' sword swaying over their relationship, ready to drop at any second and break it all up.

Ruth went up to her bedroom to lie down after clearing away her lunch things. Sunbathing was a bore now and there was little else to do. She remembered the tennis machine that served out a succession of tennis balls. Fernando had beaten her every time they played so a practice session on her own might be a good idea.

She was selecting her favourite racket in the cupboard in the hall when she heard a car coming up the drive. Not the Mercedes—she'd recognise the throaty diesel engine of Fernando's car anywhere.

Ruth hung back in the shadowy hallway and peered through the wide arched open front door, her heart beating so wildly she felt sick with it. Suppose it was Maria Luisa? A battered dusty Seat pulled up and two women got out, laughing and chatting in Spanish, and Ruth calmed herself.

The staff returning from the fiesta in Palma? Boldly Ruth stepped out into the bright sunlight, hoping her scratchy Spanish would get her through, though how she was going to explain herself she didn't know. '*Amiga de Señor Serra*' was hardly enough.

The two women grinned widely at her as she approached them and the elder of the two spoke after Ruth had tried haltingly to explain why she was here.

'*Sí, señorita, ya sé*. Hello, my English is bad. Señor Serra, he call, say you here. I am Rosa——' she nodded to the other woman, '—Dolores.' She was so proud of herself for getting that out, grinning wildly at the other woman, that Ruth couldn't subject her to more and left them for the tennis courts while they unpacked the

dusty Seat that seemed to be packed to the gunnels
with baskets of clothes and packages. So Fernando had
informed them she would be here; that sounded
encouraging.

Half an hour later Ruth was pouring with perspir-
ation and her ankle ached warningly. Mad dogs and
Englishmen and all that, she mused, glaring up at the
hot sun that glared back.

She showered and slid into her cotton robe and sat at
her dressing-table to dry her hair. It was good to hear
voices echoing around the sometimes solemn house and
the laughter of the women as they moved around
attending to their chores.

Ruth was about to switch on her blow-drier when she
stilled. She went outside to the wide corridor. The
stone-built house seemed to treble the sound. The
laughter and voices were coming from the closed rooms
at the end of the corridor that Ruth had christened the
west wing. The servants' quarters? Oh, what a fool
Fernando must have thought her for finding anything
suspicious in a locked door.

Ruth knocked on the now open door and then
stepped into the suite. She thought she ought to tell
them that she had planned to cook for Fernando
tonight. There was a main room, beautifully furnished
in soft pastels in sharp contrast to the heaviness of the
traditional furnishings in the rest of the house. Several
doors opened off from this room and Dolores came
through one. Ruth smiled in surprise at the nursery
beyond.

Dolores stood back grinning, urging Ruth to go on
in. Ruth got as far as the doorway and stopped dead.
Rosa was sitting in a white cane chair by the window,
nursing a baby in her arms. She stood up, proudly
displaying the child for Ruth to see.

She stared in amazement. A baby was the last thing
she expected to see in the servants' quarters, especially

as Rosa looked far beyond her child-bearing years. The
baby, obviously a girl in a pale pink broderie anglaise
dress, was beautiful. She must have been in one of
those baskets in the back of the car, Ruth supposed.
Before she knew it Rosa had stood up and deposited
the soft warm bundle in Ruth's arms.

'Oh, she's exquisite,' Ruth breathed ecstatically,
looking down at the little dark-haired mite swaddled in
a delicate white lace shawl, 'absolutely lovely.'

The baby's skin was a soft creamy white and her dark
lashes so long and silky they defied credibility. Her
dark hair was incredibly thick for such a small baby.
Ruth looked at Rosa questioningly. Not her child
surely, but maybe Dolores'?

'Three months,' Rosa told her proudly. '*Preciosa,
sí?*'

'Oh, *sí*, *sí*,' Ruth agreed, totally enraptured by the
child who was sleeping in her arms so peacefully. '*Cómo
se llama?*' She blushed, hoping she had got it right.
'Her name?'

Rosa laughed and looked at her as if she should
know. 'Maria Luisa, from her *madre*, Maria Luisa.'

The cool bright room spun and there was a fearful
pounding in Ruth's ears as blood rushed to her head.
She felt sick with disbelief. This couldn't be true. This
child couldn't be Maria Luisa's! Because if it was it was
also the child of. . .

The baby girl moved in her arms and blinked open
her sleepy eyes. Ruth stared down at her, barely able
to focus, and then her eyes darted frantically towards
Rosa but she had gone into the other room. The baby
gurgled and smiled and Ruth's heart tore in two.

The little mite was so like her mother, dark-haired,
dark-eyed, so beautiful that Ruth felt a deep envy grate
painfully through her, leaving her nerve-ends throbbing
with agony.

Oh, dear God, she was holding Maria Luisa's child

in her arms. Through a swell of tears Ruth stared incredulously at the bundle and felt such despair that she feared she would drop the child. Slowly, slowly, Ruth moved towards the pink cot by the wall. Gingerly she lowered the sweet-tempered child into the cot, not taking her eyes from her exquisite face, Ruth stood gripping the sides of the cot with fingers whitened in an attempt at stopping them shaking.

Tears rivered down Ruth's face till she could see no longer. This was Maria Luisa's baby and now she understood it all. It fitted like a jigsaw but her heart was fragmented into a thousand pieces.

Blindly she flew from the suite, rushed to her room and slammed shut her door and let the sobs tear out of her heart.

Maria Luisa's baby, Fernando's child! Oh, dear God, they had a baby, together they had a baby! *Preciosa, sí?* Now she understood what that something *precious* Fernando had was that would guarantee Maria Luisa returned to him instead of staying with Steve. Ruth wanted to die.

CHAPTER NINE

Two, three days? Ruth wasn't even sure how long she had been back in Palma. The drive back from Casa Pinar had been heartbreaking, passing through the villages Fernando had so excitingly guided her through days before.

But a cool, almost unnatural calm had hit her once she was back in the bustle of the city. Like a robot she'd made the calls Steve should have made and the rest of the time she had walked the city, trying to be a tourist taking in all the sights. She'd headed for the historical centre and spanned out, taking in the churches and palaces and the Lonja — the commodity exchange which housed, among other historical interests, the fine arts museum. There had been so much to see and she'd ached for Fernando to be beside her to show her everything. But her fantasies were just that — unreal. Fernando could never be a part of her life again.

Alone she wandered the shops and admired the jewellery, leather and suede and exquisite embroidery. The Manacor pearls on sale everywhere had her blinking away the tears. Though she had said she was too young for them she had been enraptured by them in a tiny jeweller's in Pollensa but Fernando had hurried her away saying he would buy her the real thing one day. At the time the offer had thrilled her, not because of the pearls but because it had indicated she would be in his life in the future. Now she knew better.

The pottery fascinated Ruth more than any other souvenirs. There was such a vast variety of decorated bowls and jugs and plates that she was spoilt for choice.

Some of it was charmingly primitive, some of it so exotically painted it took your breath away. She wanted something, though, just one small thing to take back with her. She needed a reminder of this trip even if it only served as a warning.

Ruth stood outside an open-fronted gift shop in a narrow cobbled street and gently unwrapped the clay whistle — a *siurell*, the shopkeeper had told her, an old peasant toy. It was a simple souvenir modelled in the shape of a horse and was hand-painted in red and blue and yellow. Ruth stared down at it and wondered why she had bought it and thought it was probably because it contrasted so sharply with what she had been through on this trip. There was nothing simple and primitive about her affair with Fernando. It had been riddled with complexities. The *siurell* was modest and honest somehow, unlike the man who had deceived her so.

Steve still wasn't back. Ruth fixed herself a cold drink and sat out on the balcony of the apartment to drink it. The sky was aflame and though she tried not to think of the sunsets from Fernando's cliff-top it was virtually impossible. She'd never be able to gaze in wonderment at any sunset again. It would always belong to him and he belonged to Maria Luisa and their beautiful daughter and Ruth was distraught at the thought and always would be.

Ruth could only blame herself for being so blind and gullible. She had trusted and loved him knowing Maria Luisa was a part of his life and he had never denied it. Yes, she was some prize fool.

She finished her drink and picked up a ticket wallet from the table. It contained her and Steve's return flights to England. They were for the day after tomorrow. She would be on that flight even if Steve wasn't. She couldn't wait to get away from everything that was Fernando's.

Ruth tensed as she heard a sound at the door.

Fernando? No. He wouldn't chase her after reading the letter she had left for him, politely thanking him for his hospitality and saying she was returning to Palma to complete her work before returning to England. She'd said nothing of love. It wasn't an issue any more. Fernando belonged to Maria Luisa and their child and there was no place for her in his life.

'Steve!' she cried in amazement as he let himself into the apartment, grinning all over his silly face as if he'd just popped out for a paper that morning and found he'd won the state lottery. Anger swiftly coupled with Ruth's amazement.

'Where the bloody hell have you been all this time?' she cried, throwing herself into his arms. He looked fantastic and had actually acquired quite a suntan — or was it just a glow of happiness?

Ruth's excitement, anger, hurt and every other emotion she possessed balled inside her with tension. She pushed Steve away after he had swung her around in his arms like a rag doll. 'Cool it, Steve, and tell me why you're so ecstatic. You have no reason to be. I've had to do all your work — '

'I know, sweetheart. You're an angel and I adore you and is there a bottle of champagne in the fridge because I want you to celebrate with me.' He kicked his holdall out of the way and flopped down on to the sofa, quite exhausted by whatever he had been up to since the day he left.

Ruth stared down at him in disbelief. He'd been gone so long, without a word to her on his whereabouts, and now he was back and wanting to celebrate!

'Celebrate what, for heaven's sake? Me having tied up the whole of this campaign while you've been whooping it up in Valencia — ?'

'Valencia, Alicante, Gandia — you should see the beach at Gandia, as white as I used to be — '

'Steve!' Ruth warned. He really was impossible.

'OK, so you don't want a travelogue. How does this grab you?' He was grinning from ear to ear and the first stabs of doubt needled at Ruth's heart. 'Maria Luisa and I are going to be married!'

Ruth dropped like a stone into the nearest available armchair. She had no strength left, not an ounce, not even enough to hold her eyelids up.

'Ruth?' Steve breathed worriedly.

Ruth summoned some inner strength she thought she had exhausted. She opened her eyes and gazed at him in disbelief. 'Are you crazy or what?' she squeaked.

Steve chuckled. 'Knew you'd be knocked sideways. I'm pretty chuffed myself.' He got up, galloped to the kitchen for the champagne and Ruth held her head in despair and didn't want to be there!

He came back, enthusiastically popped the cork and poured two glasses of the fizzy wine. Ruth willed it to metamorphose itself to arsenic. The whole tangled web of each other's relationships was getting to breaking-point. Now Steve wanted to marry Maria Luisa and a war was on the cards when Fernando found out!

'Where is Maria Luisa now?' Ruth asked tentatively.

Steve flopped back on to the sofa, his legs over the arm, cradling the glass of champagne in two hands. 'She's taken a taxi up to Pollensa—Casa Pinar, isn't it? I wanted to go with her but she said she had a lot to sort out with Fernando and would rather be on her own.'

'Yes, I bet she would,' Ruth muttered under her breath, then to Steve, 'But don't you mind about those two?'

'About Maria Luisa and Fernando? Of course not. They're just like you and me really—jolly good friends.'

He swigged his champagne with such abandon that Ruth knew he had swallowed Maria Luisa's explanation of their affair with the same ease as she had at first.

Ruth wondered how Maria Luisa had explained away
the baby she had conceived with her 'jolly good friend'.

'Look, Steve,' she said strongly, 'are you sure you
want to do this? I mean, it's a hell of a responsi-
bility——'

'What, marriage?' He laughed. 'Yes, it is a bit of a
step for the likes of me, I suppose, but it's what we
both want.' He grew serious. 'We're crazy about each
other and should never have been apart this last year,
but it's fate, you see, coming here and bumping into
them like that in that restaurant.' He suddenly looked
across at her. 'So how did it work out for you?'

It was such a desultory question that Ruth gave him
the filthiest look she could muster. 'What sort of a
question is that?' she scathed. 'You waltz out of here,
letting your stupid emotions rule your brain, without a
thought for me and how I was going to cope without
you——'

'But you were with Fernando——'

'You didn't know that when you waltzed off!' Ruth
snapped.

Steve scrabbled up to a sitting position and studied
her intently. 'No, I didn't, but we. . .' He hesitated,
suddenly noting the paleness of Ruth's features and the
nervous way she was swivelling her glass in her fingers.
His voice lowered a few octaves. 'Maria Luisa and I
thought it would be a good idea to get you two together
again. I told her where you would be and she told
Fernando. . .'

Ruth swallowed a small wail of despair before it got
out. Grimly she bit her lower lip. She'd been set up and
she had thought Fernando was so desperate to have her
back in his life that he had manipulated the whole
thing. He had partly, but most of it was down to
wretched Maria Luisa and conniving Steve.

'It didn't work out for you, did it?' Steve asked
reproachfully as if he didn't want to get blamed if it

hadn't. He shook his head. 'I thought. . .' He sighed,
'Maria Luisa had spoken to Fernando and you were
together at the Casa Pinar and I thought everything was
hunky-dory——'

'Hunky-dory?' Ruth exploded.

Steve looked sheepish. 'Obviously not. . . I thought
after Seville——'

With a gasp of despair Ruth slammed down the half-
empty glass of champagne and covered her face with
her hands. Almost immediately she pulled herself
together and swept her long hair from her face with
both hands. She didn't want Steve to know the terrible
truth, of what a silly fool she had been once again.
'You thought! Maria Luisa thought! You all thought
bloody wrong! It didn't work out,' she told him tightly.
'It just didn't happen for us as it so ecstatically happened for you!'

There was a long silence in which Steve weighed up
the situation before speaking. 'I'm sorry, Ruth. I'm
really sorry about that. You still care, don't you?'

Ruth waved her hand dismissively; she didn't want to
talk about it. She reached for her champagne.

'Maria Luisa will be disappointed,' Steve blundered
on, unknowing of the pain he was grinding further in.
'She said he was devastated when you went back to
England after Seville——'

'So devastated he turned to Maria Luisa for comfort?'
she bit out.

'They needed each other,' Steve said understand-
ingly. 'Maria Luisa told me all about it. How they were
a strength for each other after our affairs ended.'

Ruth stared at Steve incredulously. How could he
take this so well? She calmed herself. She had taken it
well at first herself, somehow understanding that
Fernando and Maria Luisa had drawn comfort from
each other. Then she had found out about the baby and
realised the truth—that they had done more than draw

comfort from each other as mere friends. They had loved each other, shared a life together, conceived a beautiful child together.

Sipping more wine, Ruth clutched the stem of the glass tightly. Steve was being so good about this and was willing to marry Maria Luisa in spite of the baby. . . Ruth swallowed hard and suddenly felt sick and uneasy for her bitterness. Steve was doing the right thing; he was going to marry the woman he loved even though she had a baby by another man, which was a true measure of the depth of his caring. But what would Fernando have to say about it all?

Ruth slumped back into her chair. Dear God, all this was none of her business anyway. None of it, not one small bit of it was anything to do with her. She was out on her own, not even remotely involved with their problems.

At last she spoke. 'I'm happy for you, Steve,' she told him genuinely. 'Truly happy for you.' She managed a small smile. 'So what are your immediate plans? I expect you're anxious to see little Maria Luisa.'

Steve was relieved to see her smile at his happiness, though he chuckled. 'Little? She's all of five feet five but I suppose her slim build gives the impression of being petite. . . I'm driving up to Pollensa tomorrow to pick her up and then we're flying off to Madrid to meet her parents. . . Her father is something in the government. . .' Steve looked across at Ruth who had gone deathly pale and was watching him with her mouth gaping open. 'Don't worry about the business, sweetheart, I've got it all worked out. We'll expand it into Europe. You run the UK end and I'll branch out here in Majorca. . .that's if Maria Luisa wants to go on living on the island. Ruth, what do you think?'

Ruth was already halfway across the room on her way to the balcony for air. She was shaking from head to toe, her heart thumping wildly. She wondered if this was all a dream and soon she would wake up and find they were still at Gatwick waiting to fly out to Palma. She sat down on a very solid patio chair and knew she was living a nightmare.

Steve didn't know! He didn't know about Maria Luisa's and Fernando's baby! But he must know; she must have discussed it with him. Steve being Steve was just being very laid-back about it all. 'Steve,' she called out huskily.

'More champagne?' He came out on to the balcony with the bottle and sat down next to her.

'No!' She moved her glass out of range. 'I. . . I just want to talk. . .we have to talk, Steve.' She couldn't just come out with it. It would have to come from him.

He topped up his own glass and was very silent as he did it. 'I'm sorry, Ruth,' he said sombrely. 'I'm being unfair, gabbling on about me and Maria Luisa when things didn't go right for you and Fernando. Come on, spill the beans. It will help to talk it out.'

Slowly Ruth turned her head to look at him, her partner, her friend with golden sun-bleached hair atop an open trusting face. He didn't know, he really didn't. He would have mentioned the baby by now if he had. He would have said, Didn't it work out with you and Fernando because of their baby? or something like that. She couldn't tell him; no, she couldn't. It wasn't her place to.

'It was infatuation after all for us,' she told him, putting on a brave smile. 'He was kind to look after me after you and Maria Luisa ran off into the sunset but . . .but the old magic wasn't there.' She gulped some wine and was glad of the gathering darkness now. She prayed that Steve wouldn't see the truth—that she still loved that man, passionately, even though he had deceived her so, and that her heart was breaking inside her.

'Anyway, enough of that,' she said dismissively. 'Let

me tell you what I've being doing workwise while you've been away.'

She went inside for her briefcase and Steve gave her a thoughtful look as she passed him and then polished off the remains of his champagne in one gulp.

The phone woke Ruth the next morning. Confused, she sat up in bed raking her hair from her face. She was still exhausted from the night before, shattered from trying to keep up her bravado with Steve, trying not to let slip what she knew and trying to sound enthusiastic over Steve's business plans for the future which she knew with a certainty she wanted no part of. Once off the island of Majorca she never wanted to be involved with it again.

'OK, OK!' Ruth moaned as she staggered out of her bedroom to pick up the phone. Steve was obviously out for the count.

She hesitated for a split-second before lifting the receiver. It could only be Maria Luisa asking when Steve would be leaving. She had no wish to speak to her. She might not be able to control her anger with her for deceiving Steve so, but she would have to try.

Her body went into a spasm of tension as she recognised Fernando's voice.

'Is Steve there, Ruth?'

His cool request bruised her very soul. God, it was as if nothing had ever happened between them. But of course this wasn't a personal call to her. This was to do with his mistress, their baby, and her partner Steve.

'Still sleeping. Is it important enough to drag him out of bed?' she asked sarcastically, amazed at her inner strength.

'Yes, it is, but don't,' he clipped. 'I'm sure you're quite capable of passing on a simple message. Leave a note by his bedside; you're good at that.'

'Sometimes it's the only way,' she said coldly, knowing what he was hinting at.

'The coward's way, Ruth. I expected more of you but perhaps you deserve a second chance.' His voice was cynical and Ruth wondered at what he meant. A weary frown worried her brow. She couldn't take much more. She was on the point of collapse already.

'A. . .a second chance?' she murmured hesitantly.

'Yes, while you're here supporting your partner you can tell me to my face why you intend walking out on me a second time in my life.'

Ruth wasn't sure what part of that statement she wanted to tackle first, if any. 'What do you mean, supporting my partner?'

'I think he will need your support when he gets here. He'll certainly need someone's support.'

Ruth's pulses murmured in anxiety. That sounded like a threat. 'I don't understand.'

'You will when you get here ——'

'*I'm* not coming,' Ruth told him firmly. 'This has nothing to do with me ——'

'You are a part of it,' he interrupted caustically, 'whether you like it or not, and at the moment you are the only friend Steve Cannock has and if you feel for him as you so often have claimed to you'll be at his side when he needs you.'

'And why should he need me? Steve can fight his own battles!'

Suddenly she was angry with everyone for involving her in all this. She didn't want it, didn't need it and who would be there for her when she needed a shoulder to sob on?

'This isn't a battle, Ruth ——'

'Isn't it?' Ruth blurted, fighting her tears. 'I'd say it was. You can't bear to lose Maria Luisa. So what are you going to do to Steve? Something dreadful that warrants my being at his side? I'll bring the first-aid kit with me, shall I.'

There was a long silence and then a deep sigh from Fernando and when he spoke again his voice was soft and almost at the point of exhaustion. 'I have nothing against him personally——'

'You have everything against him!' Ruth cried, the tears running down her face now. 'And. . .' her voice choked and she swallowed hard '. . .and I understand,' she went on lamely. Suddenly she felt so very deeply for him too. It must have been such a shock for him when Maria Luisa had told him she was going to marry Steve. But the baby—Steve would be shocked when he found out and perhaps Fernando was right, he did need her support.

Before she could say any more Fernando snapped impatiently, 'If you do understand then there should be no problem. Both of you be here as soon as possible.' The line went dead, giving Ruth no chance to argue.

And there was no chance for Ruth to give the conversation more thought as Steve emerged from his bedroom, tousled and bleary-eyed from too much champagne.

'What's going on?' he asked sleepily. 'Was that the phone?'

'Maria Luisa should see you now,' was the first silly remark that came to Ruth's pale lips as with trembling fingers she replaced the receiver.

'She's seen me like this every morning for over a week now,' he told her, giving her a cheeky grin, 'and still she loves me.'

Ruth turned away so he wouldn't see the torment on her face. And she was sure it was visible from the outside. Inside it raged like a swollen river. She needed time to think but there wasn't any.

'I'm coming to Pollensa with you,' she called out from the kitchen as she put the kettle on for coffee. She

gave him no explanation why; he was too befuddled
with sleep and a probable hangover for it to register
anyway, whatever she told him. And it would have had
to be a lie anyway. No way could she tell him the real
reason. She felt impelled to go. Steve would need her
but he didn't know it.

'I'm having a shower before breakfast,' Steve called
out to her, and with a sigh of relief Ruth sank to a
kitchen chair to wait for the kettle to boil. When it did
she made the coffee quickly and poured herself a cup.
She took it out to the balcony to drink it and think.

She needed the hot draught of caffeine to clear her
head. What was going to happen? Was Fernando going
to forbid Steve to marry Maria Luisa? Was he going to
ruin him as he had threatened before? Or was he going
to give them his blessing and yet refuse to give custody
of the child to Maria Luisa? Oh, yes, whatever, there
was going to be a war of sorts.

Ruth gulped the hot coffee. Poor Steve, he didn't
even know about that adorable child. Fernando was
right, he needed the support of the only friend available—herself. He had some shocks coming to him,
none of them pleasant.

On a sob Ruth swallowed hard and closed her eyes
to the burning sun overhead. And who would be there
for her at Casa Pinar where she had loved so desperately and lost so painfully? They were all so deeply
embedded in themselves there was no love or support
left for her. She was alone in the world and would have
to heal herself and somehow she would have to find the
strength to do it.

'Are you sure you want to come?' Steve asked once
again as they headed out of Palma, taking the same
route Ruth had returned to Palma by—the quickest
route. 'I said——'

'I know what you said, Steve,' she said, stretching

herself in the passenger seat, 'but I've got nothing better to do and Palma is so hot and stuffy.'

It seemed such an ineffectual reason for insisting on going with him but Steve was so wrapped up in himself and thoughts of seeing Maria Luisa again that he didn't even ask her if it might be painful for her facing Fernando again. When you were in love you only thought of yourself and your love; Ruth knew that well enough.

He chatted on about the landscape, enthusing at the sights that Ruth had already seen. He rambled on about making his home here with Maria Luisa on this wonderful island. As he got more excited as they got closer to Pollensa so Ruth sank into a deeper depression. She couldn't face Fernando again but she was going to have to and it was going to hurt her so very much.

'Take that fork,' Ruth directed and they bumped into the private road flanked by an orderly regiment of cypresses that led to the Casa.

Deeper and deeper Ruth sank till she nearly leapt out of the hired Suzuki at the gates and fled into the forest never to emerge again. How she held back she never knew.

'Wow, some place!' Steve breathed, impressed, as they trundled up the last stretch of drive after the gates had clanked shut behind them.

'A rural mansion,' Ruth mused, half to herself.

Steve gave her a sidelong glance, worried for her suddenly. 'This wasn't such a good idea, your coming, Ruth. You look thoroughly washed out.' He patted her knee. 'You've been such a brick for carrying on while I was away. Remind me to make it up to you some time. . .'

If you live, Ruth thought morbidly.

'At least you left Fernando on good terms,' he went on as he pulled up in front of the stone steps of the mansion that Ruth had fled down a century ago. 'I'll take you all out tonight, a celebratory dinner. I'm sure there are some amazing restaurants up here, some incredible *mirador* where you can see for miles and dine by moonlight.'

Ruth could think of nothing worse. Nervously she smoothed down her saffron-coloured skirt and gazed up at the house as Steve, with bounding energy, leapt out of the Suzuki. She felt so guilty for not telling him what he was in for. But in some cases ignorance was bliss. Poor darling would have enough to cope with soon enough. He was going to be told his beloved had a baby by another man and that man was probably going to threaten to ruin him. His whole world was about to collapse around his happy pink ears.

Steve was halfway up the steps, so eager to see his love once again that he didn't notice the small exclamation of shock that sprang from Ruth's full lips.

Horrified, she was glancing up at one of the windows above the porch and what she saw blanched what little remaining colour she had from her face.

Maria Luisa stood at the window, watching them arrive. Ruth had never seen such a change in anyone. She was deathly pale, her face almost swollen as if she had spent her life in tears. Her beautiful jet hair that had moved so provocatively on the yacht that night hung limp and lifeless at the side of her ashen cheeks. She looked so painfully vulnerable, almost on the edge of suicide, that Ruth's heart went out to her. What on earth had Fernando done and said to her to get her in such a state? Had he refused her permission to marry? Threatened to keep her child from her?

Shakily Ruth stepped out of the car, reaching for her raffia shoulder-bag in the back seat. She took one last glance at the window above to see Maria Luisa with her palms flat against the window-pane, desperately, mutely pleading with Ruth for help with eyes so full of pain that Ruth's nerves nearly snapped.

Ruth looked away in panic then braved herself to look back but the gaunt, pinched face had gone. She flicked her eyes to Steve standing on the porch terrace eagerly awaiting admittance to a house of horror.

She couldn't move from the bottom of the steps. Her head was spinning. She was aware of the cicadas buzzing in the heat of the day, of the sweet smell of pine trees and jasmine, her own heart thudding dully against her ribcage.

Suddenly the huge wooden arched door was sprung open and Fernando Serra stepped out of the gloom of the house and into the almost indecent brilliance of the sun.

Because of Steve standing in front of him Ruth couldn't see him properly. But what she could see was his arm leaving his side. For a fearful second she thought he was going to strike Steve but slowly he lifted his hand to reach out in greeting, not to deliver a blow.

It was then Ruth was filled with such an anger that she had to crush tight her fists to stop herself from flying up the steps to beat at Fernando's chest. Her nails bit into her palms but she felt no pain. The agony was in her heart, not just for herself but for everyone, everyone but Fernando Serra.

Through the buzz in her head she heard words spoken, formal greeting hanging in the air then she saw Steve stepping inside the house, leaving Fernando framed in the doorway.

Instinctively Ruth's hand came up to cover her mouth, to smother the gasp of shock breaking from her lips. Her wide blue eyes focused on his face and then blurred as a safety defence for something she didn't want to see.

She had been shocked by Maria Luisa's tragic countenance at the window but this was so much worse. To see a man in such a state was so much more moving. Fernando's face was grey through lack of sleep. He was clean-shaven but only just. His eyes were dark and sunken. He looked as if the world's tragedies were on his own doorstep and in a fit of hysteria Ruth supposed they were. He was anticipating losing his love and his child to Steve and it was all too much for him. Slowly he stepped across to the terrace and gazed down at her with eyes so racked with pain that Ruth's own eyes filled to the brim with her despair and lost love.

He held his hand out in a gesture for her to come into the house but in that second she knew she never could. With a small cry of anguish she took one last look at him and turned and fled.

As she headed for the path that crossed the garden to the pool and then on to the pine forest and olive grove, she heard one solitary, impassioned call that hung hauntingly in the hot air.

'Ru—th!'

The call was lost in the sound of her heart pounding furiously as she ran for the cliff-top.

CHAPTER TEN

RUTH stood on the top of the cliff-top, her skirt swirling around her trembling legs. A dry hot breeze whipped her hair and the tears from her cheeks.

She faced out to sea and saw nothing but the impression of Fernando's tortured features before her misty eyes. How long she had stood there she didn't know. Why hadn't she jumped? She had nothing to live for.

Crying Steve's name with relief, she swung round as she heard a footfall on the dry brush behind her. The breeze carried her exclamation to the man who strode towards her.

'Of course, Steve. Who else would you cry out for?'

In dismay Ruth stared at Fernando standing so gaunt and stressed in front of her. His pale grey silk shirt hung from slackened shoulders, ruffling against his chest with the same hot breeze that ruffled her own thin blouse softly against her heaving breast. She wanted to rush to him, to throw her arms around him to comfort him and for him to comfort her. She wanted him to tell her that he loved her and none of this had happened. She wanted there to be a sunset and she wanted there to be the passion and the glory and the undying love. But there could be none of that — ever again.

'I. . . I thought you were Steve,' she breathed at last when her tumbled thoughts had ceased their turmoil. She was calm now. 'It's why I'm here, don't forget, because of Steve. How is he?' she asked.

Fernando didn't move, just stood a few feet from her with dark, expressionless eyes.

'In shock,' he told her. 'Which is understandable in

the circumstances. I left them alone. They have a lot to come to terms with,' he told her desolately.

Ruth twined the fabric of her skirt in her trembling fingers at her side. She wanted to slap him for his cruelty and it was the only way to stop herself from springing at him. She raised her chin and looked at him coldly.

'You. . .you didn't hit him?' she grazed contemptuously, her eyes narrowing. 'I couldn't bear it if you hurt him.'

His own eyes narrowed. 'Why should I hit him? My heart goes out to him——'

'Liar!' Ruth blurted wildly. 'You haven't a heart! You always meant to destroy him and me——'

'Ruth?'

'Don't Ruth me. If you came up here seeking some sort of forgiveness from me you can forget it. I'll never forgive and I'll never forget!'

She went to rush past him but he caught her bare arms and swung her round, grasping her shoulders to hold her still. His touch was the last punishment. His hot hands branding her flesh for evermore was the very worst punishment of all. It seared her skin, rushed her emotions till she felt dizzy with the contact.

'Where are you going?' he grated hotly, his eyes alive now, glittering dangerously.

'To Steve, of course,' she rasped bitterly. 'That's way I'm here, that's why you summoned me here. He needs me——'

'He needs Maria Luisa now, Ruth. Let him go. . .try and let him go as easily as you let me go.'

Ruth's lips parted with shock. 'Let. . .let him go. . . let *you* go!' she whispered in disbelief. 'Steve was never *mine* to let go but I thought you were and I didn't let you go! You threw me out of your life with your treachery and your deception!' She tried to shake herself free of his grasp but his hold tightened.

His eyes were murderous now and rage coloured his pale complexion. 'Treachery and deception? When have I done anything less than love you with a passion that you chose to throw back in my face, not once but twice? Dear God, but I gave you my heart and my very soul——'

'You gave me nothing Fernando!' Ruth sobbed. 'Your heart and your soul was only ever for Maria Luisa——'

He shook her. 'You know that isn't true! You know there was nothing like that between us.'

'There was everything between you. . .everything that I thought we had. . .in Seville. . .and here. I loved you and thought you loved me——'

'I do, Ruth,' he breathed so passionately that she was almost seduced into believing him. But her reasoning cried out the truth—that he was a part of Maria Luisa and always would be. They had a bond that could never be parted, by her or Steve.

To her shock and horror his head swooped down and as his mouth claimed hers so impassionately a flash of hope surged in her heart like a spear of lightning out of a blackened sky. Her senses reeled and she fell into his arms as his lips parted hers. The force and the power of his claim on her heart rocked her. There was no fight in her, no will to stop this affray of her senses.

It was all there, the passion and the glory and inflamed rush of feeling that she knew she would always have for him. But it had no place in his life and her heart cried out in anguish.

'Oh, no. . .please don't do this to me, Fernando,' she sobbed after pulling away from him. Her eyes were as wide as a frightened fawn's as she gazed up at him. 'You know it can never be.'

'Because of your love for Steve?' he rasped angrily at her bitter betrayal. He was still clasping her by the shoulders and she tried to shake free.

'Yes, because of Steve. . .not because I love him as you think but because I care about him and. . .caring is just as emotive as loving. Now, at this very moment, he is trying to pick up the pieces of his life after you have shattered it so cruelly——'

'I've done nothing to hurt him,' Fernando argued back vehemently. 'I won't take the blame for that, not at all. Maria Luisa should have told him. She deceived him. It was her place to tell him——'

'And it was your place to tell me, Fernando,' Ruth tore out. 'That first night when we met again in the restaurant by the harbour. You should have told me that she was your life. You let her go to Steve and you shouldn't have done. You made me stay with you while they were away and you shouldn't have. You had no right, no right at all. I gave you everything too, my heart and my soul and you. . .you just used me!'

Suddenly she was free. His grip slackened and she took the opportunity to tear away from him. She stepped back, her eyes dark blue with mutiny, her fists clenched tightly at her side.

'I'm going to Steve now and I'm going to take him away from all this. You said he would need my support and that's the only thing you're right about. Neither of us deserves the pain and anguish you two have caused. We'll both get out of your lives and then you can get on with that idyllic existence you shared before we ever came to this island. You don't deserve that beautiful child of yours. . .that lovely, sweet-tempered baby. She's too good for the pair of you; she doesn't deserve such treachery from her parents!'

She turned and ran then, blindly, not knowing where she was going. Suddenly she was grasped from behind and the sky swam all around her as she fell heavily to the ground, landing with Fernando half across her.

She fought him, desperately, clawing and pummelling at him and shrieking out every obscenity she knew. She

fought him till there was no strength left. Limply she
fell back against the unyielding scrubland, sobbing and
crying, numb to everything but Fernando's flutter of
consoling kisses across her face and throat.

'Shush now, *querida*, my love, my life.'

'You bastard!' she cried. 'I hate you, I hate you!'

'You don't hate,' he soothed. 'You love, you love me
and no other and I love you and no other. I never have
and I never will.'

'And you're a liar!' Ruth scathed, her chest heaving
so hard she could scarcely catch her breath. 'You love
no one. I don't even think you love Maria Luisa or your
child. You don't know what love is! You're nothing but
a cheater!'

'And you are a delightful, adorable, blind idiot.' He
had the audacity to smile and Ruth squirmed frantically
under him but he stilled her thrashing body with the
weight of his own. 'How could you believe that of me,
Ruth? You, dear Ruth, with your successful company,
your beauty, your intelligence, how could you let your
sensibility come up with the very idea that Maria Luisa's
baby is mine?'

Ruth felt as if a blow had been delivered to her ribs
with a mallet. Her breath went and left her gasping for
air. She struggled for life in a dizzy world of red fire
and molten lead. She fought her way up out of the
catharsis, every nerve in her weak, weak body fighting
for life.

'Fernando!' she cried at last, struggling to sit up.

Fernando eased her back to the ground, smoothed
her tear-dampened hair from her flushed cheeks. 'Yes,
I'm here and I always will be. Just for you and only
you, My poor, poor darling. Did you believe, really
believe that baby Maria Luisa was mine?'

Ruth struggled for words, her mind so confused that
she couldn't rein a coherent thought to the surface.

What was he saying? She didn't understand, she just didn't.

His mouth caressed hers, sensuously, tenderly, trying to soothe her confusion. Small kisses, so sweet and conciliatory, running over her upper lip, across her face, down her throat.

'Please, Fernando,' she pleaded. 'Please tell me that it's true. Tell me again and again. Tell me the baby isn't yours.'

'It isn't mine, dear Ruth. It could never be mine. How could you ever believe that?'

'But. . .but you're living with her. You said and. . .'

'I said we lived together and that is true, not as lovers, though. I told you it wasn't that sort of relationship. But I couldn't say more. It wasn't my place to indulge to anyone, even you who I adore. You must understand that, Ruth. I never intended to cheat you as you accused. I told you all I was at liberty to and thought you had accepted it.'

'I. . . I did,' Ruth insisted, catching her breath. 'I did believe you. I wouldn't have stayed otherwise. I wouldn't have allowed our love to rekindle otherwise but. . .'

'But what, *querida*?' What made you so suddenly doubt me?'

'Oh, God,' Ruth breathed with such distress that Fernando tightened his grip around her, folding her so hard into his tense body that she clung to him hotly. 'I was so afraid, all the time I was here with you. It was always in the back of my mind. You and Maria Luisa. You. . .you assured me she wasn't a part of your life and I did. . . I did believe you but you. . .you were never really honest with me. Every time I asked you——'

'I couldn't tell you the truth, Ruth. it wasn't my secret to divulge. Maria Luisa made me swear I would never tell anyone and I did because she needed to trust

someone. She was lost and alone and lived in fear of
her parents ever finding out she had a baby.'

Ruth buried her face in his neck and fought back the
tears for poor Maria Luisa. 'Oh, Fernando, I don't
know what to say.' She clasped his face between her
hands, his wonderful, handsome, oh, so stressed face,
smoothing her fingers across the planes of his skin. 'The
day you went to meet your lawyer. . .' She faltered,
wondering if she could speak the devastation she had
felt when Rosa and Dolores had shown her that tiny
baby. She swallowed hard. It must come out, all her
fears. 'Rosa and. . .and Dolores came back to the
house. They seemed. . .seemed to know me. They said
they knew I was there. I thought it was all going to be
all right. I was always afraid that once Maria Luisa
returned you would choose her rather than me.'

'How could you think that, *querida*? You must have
known how deeply I loved you. There was Seville and
then the wonderful fate that brought us together again.
I thought you were happy here on my island, that you
loved me and wanted to stay with me.'

'You never asked me, though. I kept waiting and
waiting for you to ask me to stay but you didn't. I
thought you were still mad at me for carrying on my
work and then I thought you were just waiting for
Maria Luisa to come back before. . .oh, before making
your decision. . .'

Fernando was about to protest but Ruth stilled his
lips with the tips of her fingers.

'Let me finish, my darling, because I have to. I have
to tell you the terrible things I thought about you when
I stumbled into that nursery, part of the rooms you had
locked away from me. Rosa was holding the baby, by
the window. I hadn't seen them carry her in from the
car so it was a terrible shock for me. I can't speak much
Spanish and Rosa speaks little English but. . .but some-

how we managed. I asked about the baby and she looked at me as if I should know.'

Ruth paused to draw breath, gazing up into Fernando's dark eyes, praying he would understand. He was looking down at her so fondly and with such deep understanding that she was encouraged to go on.

'Rosa said she was called Maria Luisa. . .like her mother. . .and. . .and my whole world fragmented. I thought I understood it all then. I imagined you let her go away with Steve because you. . .you thought she would finally get him out of her system, and you did say that you were certain she would return as you had something precious that Steve hadn't got. Rosa used the word *preciosa* to describe the baby and the association was made. I suddenly understood, or thought I understood it all. That baby Maria Luisa was that something precious that would bring Maria Luisa back to you.'

'And she is precious to Maria Luisa and yes, I was certain she would return — because of the baby, not me.'

'I know. . . I see that now,' Ruth whispered. She felt the tears stinging her eyes again, for herself and her shame. 'I was so insecure, Fernando. I had lost you once before because of my stupidity but now here was something else that completely undermined me — a tiny baby, a hold over you that I could never compete with. I ran away, back to Palma, because I couldn't bear the pain of Maria Luisa coming back, wanting you back and the life all three of you shared.'

Fernando stroked her silky hair and kissed her forehead. 'My poor darling. If you had waited for me to return and confronted me with your distress I would have told you. I'd have gone against Maria Luisa and broken my vow of silence to put you out of your misery. For so long I'd managed to hold off your curiosity but I was near to breaking-point. Rosa and Dolores were

looking after the child in Palma and I knew they were
due to return. The strain was enormous.'

'You were strange with me the last days and I was
being so awful. I was so afraid of losing you to Maria
Luisa, dreading her return, then it was just too terrible
when I thought you were the father of her baby.'

He shook his head for the pain she had been through.
'When I got back and found your note I didn't think for
a minute that it was because you thought I was the
father of the child. It never occurred to me you could
think that. Rosa told me you had been enthralled with
the baby, how adorable you thought she was. I didn't
think your disappearance was connected. I just
thought. . .'

'You just thought that once again I was putting my
business and. . .and Steve before my love for you.'

He kissed her mouth, possessively, then drew back
to mouth his answer across her lips. 'I didn't think of
anything for a good few hours,' he admitted throatily.
'I was numb with shock. Then I was angry and felt
cheated. Yes, eventually I did put it down to your job,
worried about Steve being so long away and anxious to
tie up the contract, but there was a worse fear—that
you just didn't love me enough to want to stay with
me.'

'Oh, I do love you, Fernando,' Ruth cried passionately. 'I always did but it isn't easy, is it? Loving, I
mean. It's full of so many doubts and worries and fear.
I know we said it so many times in Seville but even then
there was that feeling it was so unreal. You admitted
that yourself.'

'Only to cover my own insecurity in case you rejected
me once again.'

'You still believe I rejected you the first time, don't
you?' Ruth asked uncertainly.

He put her mind at rest with a sweet tender kiss on
her lips. 'We were both at fault, *querida*. You shouldn't

have doubted the depth of my love for you but I understand why you felt so insecure. Seville was another world for us both. But I should never have let you slip away so easily. I should have been on the following flight to bring you back. For days, weeks, I was too indecisive to do anything, thinking that once home your love would fade——'

'It never did, Fernando; not for one second did I have any doubts of how deeply I felt for you, only doubts of how deeply you had felt for me. I just thought that you would come after me and when you didn't. . . I just thought. . .'

'I would have come, you know. Eventually I wouldn't have been able to stop myself.'

'But you didn't,' Ruth murmured sadly. 'You didn't come for me, Fernando.'

Again he chased away her fears with a tender kiss that had her melting against him. 'Then I was too late,' he murmured against her mouth. He drew back from her then and studied her misty blue eyes. 'Maria Luisa needed me so badly, Ruth. She was in a terrible state. Try and understand the position I was in. I've known her all her life. My father was a great friend of her father. When she started flying her parents asked me to keep a watchful eye on her. She was on domestic routes and we often met up, like in Seville. She often stayed in my homes. I was the first person she turned to when she found herself pregnant.'

'Couldn't she have turned to her parents?'

Fernando shook his head and smiled ruefully. 'Remember what I told you about her family? Her father's a politician, her mother a charity worker.'

'Charity begins at home,' Ruth suggested wryly at the same time uncharitably thinking that Maria Luisa must have put Fernando under such a terrible strain over something that had nothing to do with him.

'Tell that to the only child of a respected Madrid

family who'd already gone against her parents' wishes to fly.'

Ruth's heart softened. 'She must have been distraught.'

'She was, desperate. I tried to persuade her to go home, even suggested I go with her to talk to her parents but she couldn't even face that. She just pleaded with me to let her stay with me till the baby was born and then she would try and gather the courage to tell her family.'

'And. . .and she hasn't yet?'

Fernando shook his head. Suddenly he sat up, drew his legs up and leaned his elbows on his knees. He gazed out to sea. Slowly Ruth sat up too and leaned her head against his shoulder.

'And you've had to live with this, knowing what she was doing was wrong and yet showing such concern for her. Oh, Fernando, you're such a beautiful person. You make me feel so bad for ever doubting you, for thinking you and she were lovers. You looked after her all that time and you're still looking after her.' A thought crossed her mind and her lips thinned contemptuously. 'But what about the father of the child? Oh, God, I bet he was some married creep who didn't want to know. Men can be such bastards. . .'

Fernando turned to look at her and she lifted her head from his shoulder to stare wildly out to the horizon, so engrossed with yet another disturbing thought she didn't notice the curious expression on his face.

'Oh, Fernando —— ' she turned her face to his ' — now I know what you meant when you called this morning — that Steve would need a friend, need my support.' She bit her lip fiercely. 'Oh, God, poor Maria Luisa, poor, poor Steve. I saw her at the window when we arrived. She looked suicidal and there was Steve so happy, so in love. . .' Suddenly her eyes filled with tears. 'Oh,

Fernando. He loves her so much and what's he going through now she has told him she has a child by another man?'

Steve would feel exactly as she had felt when she had thought Fernando was the father of that child — absolute desolation. There had been no one there for her when she had made that terrible discovery. She had borne it all alone, not knowing it wasn't true. But she was here for Steve and she wouldn't let him down.

She tried to struggle to her feet, pulling at her skirt that was half under Fernando. 'I've got to go to him, Fernando. You're right, he needs me. He's going to be devastated. . . Fernando, let me go. . . Fernando!'

He was trying to pull her back down to the ground and laughing in disbelief as he did it.

She struggled to stay on her feet. 'Oh, it isn't funny, Fernando——'

'But it is, my sweet, sweet idiot, and I find it hard to believe you don't know——'

'Don't know what?' she cried, angry with him for not sympathising with Steve at this awful time of his life. 'That at this very minute Maria Luisa is telling him she can't marry him because she has a child by another man? You said he was in shock——'

'And he is, a delighted shock——'

'Delighted! He must be devastated!' she cried furiously.

'Well, that as well. Ecstatic too when he sees his baby daughter for the first time.'

The world spun. The whole world turned on its axis and dumped Ruth back down on the ground with a thump. Incredulously she stared at Fernando's grinning face as he took her gently by the shoulders.

'His daughter!' she croaked in disbelief. Fernando never said a word, just smiled at her ashen features as her mouth started to quiver. 'Steve's daughter? His baby? Maria Luisa's baby is his?

Suddenly the tears were there, brimming from her eyes with joy and happiness and such relief. 'Oh, Fernando,' she spluttered, lowering her head with shame. 'I am stupid, aren't I? Such a blind, blind, silly fool!' She covered her face with her hands and sobbed and sobbed. He held her shoulders and through her cries of anguish she heard Fernando's sudden worried question.

'Ruth, darling, you didn't. . .you didn't tell Steve on the way here that. . .that the child was. . .was mine?'

Suddenly the anguish was gone and she was laughing and crying at the same time. She let her hands slide from her face. 'Oh, thank God, I didn't. I never said a word. I couldn't, I was in such a turmoil. I knew Steve didn't know about the baby. When he arrived back last night he was so happy about his love and wanting to marry Maria Luisa I couldn't burst his bubble so soon. When we arrived I couldn't come into the house because I knew. . .thought I knew what was coming. When I saw Maria Luisa's distress at the window I thought it was all over for him and. . .and when you opened the door looking so terrible yourself I thought you had told her you wouldn't give her custody of the baby. Oh, Fernando, it was nothing like that, was it?'

'Nothing like that at all,' he agreed. 'She was upset because I nearly lost my temper with her. When she arrived back I found out that she still hadn't told Steve. From the very start I had advised her to be honest with him but she was terrified he would be so shocked he wouldn't want her. He phoned her after Seville but she never called him back because almost immediately she found she was pregnant. I tried to reason with her that he should know about the baby but she refused to call back or write to him. She said she didn't want that sort of hold over him.'

'But now, after their time together on the mainland, she must have known he truly loved her,' Ruth insisted.

'She did, but it got worse for her. When you hold something back for so long it's always harder. By the time he proposed it was impossible. She had let it go too far. She just completely lost her nerve and was too afraid to tell him for fear of rejection. We were up most of the night. I thought she had matured this past year with me but all my hard work to get her to face up to her responsibilities crumbled when Steve came back on the scene.'

Ruth ran her fingers over his face. 'You looked so awful earlier, so gaunt and haunted. You must really care for her.'

'I care more for you, *querida*. If I look so bad it's because I thought I had lost you. All the time I was reasoning with Maria Luisa I was thinking I should be reasoning with you, trying to win you back. I've spent the last year of my life caring for the wrong person.'

'Maria Luisa needed you,' Ruth said kindly.

'But you needed me more, Ruth. You needed to be reassured of my love for you. My last chance was today, by insisting you come here with Steve.'

'I might not have come,' she teased lightly.

'I made it happen. I willed you to come and you did and now you are here and I'm never going to let you out of my sight again. I'm going to love you and make love to you till the sunset ceases to happen.'

'That's forever, to eternity and the end of the world,' Ruth murmured lovingly.

'So it shall be,' he breathed heatedly as his hands moved to unbutton her blouse. His mouth closed over hers with the passion and glory she knew would never die and she melted into his impassioned embrace with a heart that was free to be his at last.

Her blouse fell open and her naked breast was warmed by the hot sun and his mouth drawing her desire from deep within her, a desire she thought had been lost for no other man would have been able to free it, no other but him.

'I love you,' she moaned deeply as his hands caressed her.

'And I love you, my beautiful Ruthie, and you'll never run from my love again because we are going to be married, as soon as possible, and Majorcan wives never leave their husbands. I'm going to keep a short rope on you for the rest of our lives.'

'Like your goat and your mule?' she teased.

'And in that order too,' he whispered heatedly. 'You will marry me, won't you, my only love?'

'Oh, Fernando, yes, I'll marry you.' She clung to him, passionately rained kisses down his face, easing the anguish, careering her hands down his back as he moved restlessly against her.

Minutes later he was loving her completely, his thrusts deep inside her, his penetration so absolute, so wonderfully possessive that she closed around him instinctively, holding him where he belonged, within her for evermore.

She grasped his hips into hers, never to let him go, and he responded with the rhythm of love she craved so strongly.

'And there isn't even a sunset yet,' she husked desperately as the fire of his body and his need for her swelled and swelled within her till she was writhing with sweet ecstasy beneath him on the dry, dusty cliff-top.

'When we love like this the passion and the glory is within, *querida*.'

And then she knew it was true as, under the hot Mediterranean sun, their love was sealed for eternity in that final last desperate burst of flame and fire that heralded not the end of a wonderful Majorcan day but the beginning of their life and love together.

Welcome to Europe

MAJORCA

At sixty miles long and covering 1405 square miles, Majorca is the largest of the Balearic Islands, with a distinctive diversity in its landscape and atmosphere. Beaches and fertile plains contrast with the mountainous region which extends from the south-west to the northern tip of the island, so that, whatever your mood and inclination, Majorca has plenty to offer. Whether you and your lover are the sunbathing sort or keen explorers and sightseers — or both! — in surroundings like these you are guaranteed a memorable and happy holiday.

THE ROMANTIC PAST

In the third century B.C. Majorca was captured by the Carthaginians, who in turn were defeated by the Romans in 146 B.C. However, the islanders managed to escape Roman occupation until 123 B.C. when the islands were given the names **Balearis Major** (now Majorca) and **Balearis Minor** (Minorca). Successive invasions by Vandals and Goths eventually supplanted

Roman power, until the Moors took control in the early tenth century.

It wasn't until 1229 that **Jaime I of Aragon**—James the Conqueror—managed to drive the Moors out of Majorca and the island was established as an independent Christian kingdom.

With the death of the Spanish dictator Franco in 1975, **King Juan Carlos I** introduced democracy, which led to a renaissance of the unique languages and cultures of the Balearic Islands so that once again they could enjoy their regional identity.

Legend has it that when **King Jaime I** approached Majorca by sea in 1229 he encountered a dreadful storm, and, fearing for his life, swore that should he survive he would build a church dedicated to St Mary. Consequently he donated the land on which the famous **La Seo** cathedral in Palma was built, although the building was not finished until 1601.

In about 1265 the scholar and poet **Ramón Llull** is said to have ridden his charger up the steps of the church on **Plaza Santa Eulalia** in **Palma**, in pursuit of a woman who had caught his eye. When she revealed her diseased breasts to him he immediately took holy orders and became a monk!

The **Caves of Drach** were one of the five official gateways to the ancient underworld and the last High Priestess of the Mother Cult held court there.

Famous people who have visited Majorca include Chopin and George Sand, Robert Graves, Picasso, and Winston Churchill.

THE ROMANTIC PRESENT — pastimes for lovers. . .

A logical place to begin sightseeing in Majorca is
Palma, the island's capital. By far the best way of seeing
the historical sights of the city is on foot, but a leisurely
ride in one of the local horse-drawn cabs known as
galera is also to be recommended if you would rather
conserve your energy! Nearly two-thirds of Majorca's
population live in Palma, and it is always buzzing with
visitors, but don't let this deter you, because there are
plenty of sights worth seeing.

The Palacio de Almudaina was once the residence of
the Moorish kings and now serves as headquarters of
the Captain-General of Majorca. Inside is a museum
containing many interesting artefacts, antique furniture
and Flemish tapestries depicting Spanish history.

Palma's majestic Gothic cathedral, **La Seo**, is one of
Spain's most famous landmarks and inside it is breath-
takingly beautiful, with its numerous stained-glass windows and rose window — said to be the largest in the
world — throwing multi-coloured light across the free-
standing columns which support the central nave's roof.
The kings of Majorca are buried here, and the treasury
contains a jewel-studded crucifix, gold and enamel
work, tapestries and thirteenth-century paintings.

If you now head towards the harbour on the **Pont y
Vich P Nadal** you will come across the **Museo de
Mallarco**, housed in a seventeenth-century palace and
containing several sculptures, Moorish ceramics, paintings and artefacts. Just behind this building are the **Arab
Baths**, one of very few Arab structures in the city sur-
viving in its original form. Inside are two chambers —
the *calderium*, for steam bathing, and the *tepiderium*,

for cold baths. The baths were used by rich Arabs in much the same way that saunas are used today.

For a wonderful example of aristocratic Majorcan architecture be sure to visit the **Palacio Vivot**, now a national monument. Don't be fooled by the rather austere Gothic exterior—inside you will find a magnificent museum of antique furniture, maps, paintings and silver.

Also worth visiting is **La Lonja**, one of the grandest civic buildings in the world. Once Palma's stock exchange, it is thought that Christopher Columbus might have traded here; today the building is used to exhibit art, some of which dates back to the fourteenth century.

As you wander around, other notable buildings to look out for are **La Consolat del Mar** (Admiralty Court), an impressive seventeenth-century edifice containing maritime exhibits, and the **Ayuntamiento** (old town hall)— a three-storeyed Renaissance structure and fine example of Majorcan architecture.

In addition, no visit to Palma would be complete without admiring the wonderful views from the battlements of the fourteenth-century **Castillo Bellver**—a masterpiece of Gothic building standing 450 feet above sea level.

As far as shopping is concerned, Palma is bound to pull at your purse-strings! You can find shops of every kind here, plus several markets and bazaars (but be sure to haggle!) where you can buy all manner of souvenirs. Majorca is famous for **leather** and **suede** goods—particularly shoes—**pottery** and **ceramics** are abundant, as are **jewellery** and **basketwork**. The famous **artificial**

pearls from Manacor are good value for money, but one of the most popular gifts is the *siurell* — a handmade and painted clay figure with a built-in whistle!

Of course Majorca has a great reputation for fine beaches, and there are plenty to choose from if you fancy a spot of sunbathing. The most popular and therefore the most crowded tend to be to the south and west of the island — for example at **El Arenal**, **Palma Nova** and **Magalluf** — but there is a lovely unspoilt beach to the east of the island at **Playa de Canyamel** and at **Cala Murada**. But if you really want to soak up the sun in a quieter atmosphere you should head north to either **Puerto Pollença** — one of the island's most attractive resorts — or to **Cala San Vicente**, where there are two small beaches connected by a concrete pathway and only a few bars and shops.

Once you are well rested and nicely sun-kissed it's time to take in some sights round the rest of the island. Worth visiting is **Valldemossa**, where you will find Robert Graves' house and **La Cartuja** — the Carthusian monastery where, in 1838, **Frédéric Chopin** and his French authoress lover **George Sand** spent the winter. It was here that Chopin composed some of his finest works, and Sand wrote her book **A Winter in Majorca**. So if you're a music-lover a trip to the monastery's cell No. 2, where the couple lived, is a must.

Alternatively, if you're feeling energetic, head for the famous **Calvari** at **Pollensa**. Here you'll find an enormous stairway of 365 steps amid cypress trees, leading to a little church which overlooks the town. The scenic views are breathtaking and well worth the climb — honestly!

However, arguably the most spectacular scenery on
Majorca is to be found at the **Formentor Peninsula** —
the view from the lighthouse at **Cabo Formentor**, at the
northernmost point of the island, is fantastic. And while
you're here, for a real romantic treat, why not take
afternoon tea or a cooling drink at the fabulous **Hotel
Formentor**? It is very luxurious, and was the first hotel
to be built on the island — in the 1920s.

In contrast, near **Ponto Cristo** are the **Cuevas del Drach**
(Caves of the dragon) — a major tourist attraction, and
very impressive. A boat trip will take you into the
caverns, where the magnificent limestone formations
are reflected in the crystal-clear water by special lighting
effects, and the stalagmites and stalactites give added
dramatic effect. One of the highlights of the tour is the
large underground **Lago Martel**, where torchlit musical
concerts are performed daily from boats on the lake's
still waters.

Where food is concerned Majorca has plenty of local
specialities on offer, as well as the classic Spanish dishes
such as *paella*, *gazpacho* and *tapas*. The Majorcans
don't bother much with breakfast; usually they have
just a cup of coffee and perhaps an *ensaimada* — a light
fluffy spiral of pastry sometimes filled with cream,
almonds or fruit. For lunch try a *coco* — a small pizza
filled with vegetables, fish or something sweet, *pa amb
oli* — bread spread with fresh tomatoes and seasoned
with salt and olive oil, or *sobrasada* — seasoned pork
sausage similar to pâté which is eaten spread on *pan
payés* (bread).

For a more substantial evening meal you might like to
try *lechona* — roast suckling pig and Majorca's traditional dish for celebrations. Tasty alternatives include
escaladun — casserole of chicken and turkey with

potatoes and almonds, **calderata langosta** — lobster pieces in a thick tomato-based sauce, and **tubet** — peppers, tomatoes, aubergine, potato and pumpkin fried in oil.

The best wines come from the mainland — **Rioja** and **Penedés**, for example — but the dark red Majorcan **Binissalem** wine is worth trying. One of the most famous of Majorcan drinks is **palo** — a slightly bitter liqueur flavoured with crushed almond shells, and there are also herb-based local liqueurs called **hierbas**, which are very popular.

DID YOU KNOW THAT. . .?

* during the tourist season the population of Majorca can swell from 325,000 to 500,000.

* the dozens of **palm trees** which give the island's capital its name were probably introduced from Africa during the Arab occupation of Majorca.

* exports include **leather shoes** and **artificial pearls**.

* the currency of Majorca is the **peseta**.

* the Spanish way to say 'I love you' is *'Te amo'*, *'Te adoro'* or *'Te quiero'*.

LOOK OUT FOR TWO TITLES EVERY MONTH IN OUR SERIES OF EUROPEAN ROMANCES:

WEST OF BOHEMIA: Jessica Steele (Czechoslovakia)
On a mission to help her sister, Fabia travelled to Czechoslovakia to try and interview the arrogant Ven Gajdusek. But would he see through her deception?

SICILIAN SPRING: Sally Wentworth (Sicily)
Bryony had sworn off men — but could she resist Rafe Cavalleri's devastating Italian charm?

SUDDEN FIRE: Elizabeth Oldfield (Portugal)
Vitor d'Arcos seemed determined to make Ashley want him — second time around. But this time Ashley had her son to think of. . .

LOVE'S REVENGE: Mary Lyons (Corsica)
Xavier believed that Louisa's brother owed him a debt . . .only the arrogant Corsican seemed determined that Louisa should be the one to pay it!

Accept 4 FREE Romances and 2 FREE gifts

FROM READER SERVICE

Here's an irresistible invitation from Mills & Boon. Please accept our offer of 4 FREE Romances, a CUDDLY TEDDY and a special MYSTERY GIFT! Then, if you choose, go on to enjoy 6 captivating Romances every month for just £1.80 each, postage and packing FREE. Plus our FREE Newsletter with author news, competitions and much more.

Send the coupon below to: Mills & Boon Reader Service, FREEPOST, PO Box 236, Croydon, Surrey CR9 9EL.

NO STAMP REQUIRED

Yes!
Please rush me 4 FREE Romances and 2 FREE gifts! Please also reserve me a Reader Service subscription. If I decide to subscribe I can look forward to receiving 6 brand new Romances for just £10.80 each month, post and packing FREE. If I decide not to subscribe I shall write to you within 10 days - I can keep the free books and gifts whatever I choose. I may cancel or suspend my subscription at any time. I am over 18 years of age.

Ms/Mrs/Miss/Mr _____ EP55R

Address _____

_____

Postcode _____ Signature _____

MAILING PREFERENCE SERVICE

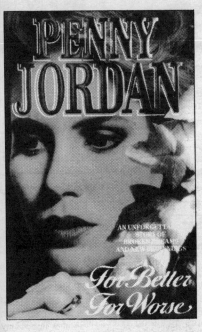

Next Month's Romances

Each month you can choose from a wide variety of romance with Mills & Boon. Below are the new titles to look out for next month, why not ask either Mills & Boon Reader Service or your Newsagent to reserve you a copy of the titles you want to buy – just tick the titles you would like and either post to Reader Service or take it to any Newsagent and ask them to order your books.

Please save me the following titles:	Please tick	√
DAWN SONG	Sara Craven	
FALLING IN LOVE	Charlotte Lamb	
MISTRESS OF DECEPTION	Miranda Lee	
POWERFUL STRANGER	Patricia Wilson	
SAVAGE DESTINY	Amanda Browning	
WEST OF BOHEMIA	Jessica Steele	
A HEARTLESS MARRIAGE	Helen Brooks	
ROSES IN THE NIGHT	Kay Gregory	
LADY BE MINE	Catherine Spencer	
SICILIAN SPRING	Sally Wentworth	
A SCANDALOUS AFFAIR	Stephanie Howard	
FLIGHT OF FANTASY	Valerie Parv	
RISK TO LOVE	Lynn Jacobs	
DARK DECEIVER	Alex Ryder	
SONG OF THE LORELEI	Lucy Gordon	
A TASTE OF HEAVEN	Carol Grace	

If you would like to order these books in addition to your regular subscription from Mills & Boon Reader Service please send £1.80 per title to: Mills & Boon Reader Service, Freepost, P.O. Box 236, Croydon, Surrey, CR9 9EL, quote your Subscriber No:................................... (If applicable) and complete the name and address details below. Alternatively, these books are available from many local Newsagents including W.H.Smith, J.Menzies, Martins and other paperback stockists from 3 December 1993.

Name:...

Address:..

....Post Code:.........................

To Retailer: If you would like to stock M&B books please contact your regular book/magazine wholesaler for details.

You may be mailed with offers from other reputable companies as a result of this application. If you would rather not take advantage of these opportunities please tick box ☐